EBURY PRESS

CAN WE BE STRANGERS AGAIN?

Shrijeet Shandilya is a writer who discovers stories in the smallest moments, lingering discussions, spoken silences and memories that refuse to fade. He finished his undergraduate studies at Christ University, Bengaluru, and is currently pursuing his MBA at the Goa Institute of Management. Somewhere between surviving deadlines and making sense of it all, he discovered his love for writing. His writing incorporates comedy, nostalgia and passion, portraying the bittersweetness of growing up, moving on and everything in between. His debut novel *Can We Be Strangers Again?* is a reflection of these emotions—love, loss and the spaces in between them. You may reach him at shrijeet104@gmail.com.

can
we be
strangers
again?

SHRIJEET SHANDILYA

EBURY
PRESS

An imprint of Penguin Random House

EBURY PRESS

Ebury Press is an imprint of the Penguin Random House group of
companies whose addresses can be found at global.penguinrandomhouse.com

Published by Penguin Random House India Pvt. Ltd
4th Floor, Capital Tower 1, MG Road,
Gurugram 122 002, Haryana, India

First published in Ebury Press by Penguin Random House India 2025

ISBN 9780143475927

Typeset in Sabon LT Std by MAP Systems, Bengaluru, India
Printed at Thomson Press India Private Limited

www.penguin.co.in

To Tam, the calm in my storms.
To Avantika, the mirror that showed me my worth.

And to you, dear reader,
may you lose yourself in these pages
only to find a piece of your soul waiting at the end.

A New Beginning in Uncertain Times

It was a rainy day in Goa. I sat on my balcony, taking in the pouring rain. The air was heavy with petrichor, and a strange sense of calm enveloped me. I lit a cigarette; the glowing tip of it stood out against the grey backdrop like a small, warm orange ember.

The rain had a way of washing everything clean, but today, it only seemed to stir up what I'd tried to bury.

Suddenly I felt a vibration in my pocket. I thought to myself that it would be just another college-related message. But something in my heart told me to check the notification. And there it was! My heart skipped a beat as I read the message. '**Can we be strangers again?**'

I felt a familiar ache, like an old wound reopening. I let out a deep sigh, trying to push the phone back into my pocket, just like the old memories, and engulfed myself in thoughts of my past filled with extreme emotions of ecstasy and doubt.

Every detail from my past—the lows, the highs—reminded me of her, the girl who touched my heart so deeply. Her presence was a mix of happiness and heartache and, even though it left a scar, it was beautiful in its own painful way.

'She helped shape the person I am today,' I thought, feeling a strange blend of nostalgia and longing.

The rain thundered steadily, like a familiar rhythm panning the quiet echoes of my memories. I smiled a little, feeling how we would laugh at the simplest of things, and how she would make the darkest days bearable. But as quickly as that, the sadness stepped back in; and with it, the memory of the day when everything had changed came rushing back—the day I learnt that some moments leave a scar that never fades.

It all started in 2020, a year that seemed to set the stage for so many changes and new chapters in my life. Something I didn't know back then. I had no idea then that it would change everything, and shape me in ways I never imagined.

Now, in 2024, I see how those moments from 2020 laid the groundwork for everything.

Let's take a trip back to 2020, where it all started.

It was the year I was excited to attend Christ University. One of the top commerce colleges in India, after all! I imagined entering this pulsating campus full of new people I would have been friends with.

But then, God had other plans! COVID arrived and changed everything.

The pandemic meant I was part of the 'COVID batch', which also meant starting college from my room. On the first day, I sat at my desk, waiting for my online class to start. It wasn't exactly the college experience I had imagined—no crowded lecture halls, no excited chatter. Just me, and a screen filled with tiny faces.

It felt strange and a bit lonely. While I was looking forward to the classroom energy, suddenly the classroom came to my home in the online mode and that doomed my chances of meeting new people. Now, I had to make friends through this new medium and even learn through it, which was a new and challenging task.

To break the ice, the college started a WhatsApp group for all the new students. I watched as the group filled up with random numbers and introductions.

Akinchan, a guy from Ghaziabad, took the initiative to start a conversation.

'Hey everyone!' he typed, introducing himself. His enthusiasm made a difference, and slowly, the group started warming up. But not everyone was responsive. Some people simply read the messages but didn't reply.

Even though it was a slow start, I held on to the hope that once everything was back to 'normal' again, we would all finally have the chance to connect in person. I wanted to meet everyone, build real connections, even if it took time.

The Spirit of Christ University

Even though finding that new routine was a task, I was far more nervous about starting a new journey at Christ.

The virtual setting was quite new but felt really special as we introduced ourselves yet again. As I logged in and faces began to pop up on the screen, we were greeted by Dr (Fr) Jossy P. George, the university director. His presence, a blend of warmth and authority, stood out amidst the usual WebEx monotony.

With a warm smile and a rich, husky voice, he said, 'Good morning, Christites.' His greeting carried a deep sense of pride and belonging. 'I know this year is different, but once a Christite, always a Christite. The spirit of Christ is in our blood.'

Eventually, we came to know of the Christ anthem. The anthem, with its stirring lyrics and powerful melody, prominently featured the call: 'March on, Christites.' Even sitting back at home, the lyrics gave us goosebumps. The anthem was a reminder of our united identity, stirring a deep sense of pride and connection.

As we gradually fell in love with the university's traditions, it became clear that being a Christite was more than just attending college; it was making your alma mater a part of you, no matter where you were or how things changed.

The First Class and the Unexpected Task

As I logged into WebEx, a mix of nervousness and anticipation swirled within me. And then, she appeared on our screens—Manjari Ma'am.

'Good morning, students!' she said with her warm voice; it literally felt like a hug for a second.

Well, all I can say is that most of the boys in the class were already flattered.

'All right, let's get into today's problem,' Manjari Ma'am said, as she manoeuvred through her slides.

I groaned inwardly, but it was high time I faced my fear of Mathematics.

Mayur, sitting next to me in the virtual room, was also clearly struggling. 'I don't get this at all,' he typed in the chat. 'Is it just me?'

'Nope, I'm lost too,' Akinchan replied. 'But let's hang in there. She's supposed to be good.'

Just as we were getting wrapped up in the numbers, Manjari Ma'am dropped a surprise. 'Just so you know,' she mentioned casually, 'I'm married and have a child.'

The string of words fell upon us like rain on dry ground, waking us up from our daydreams. The room went silent with a stunned sort of silence, and the elaborate fantasy we'd built around her lay in ruins. It was sobering to think that the person we honoured and admired so much had a full and happy life outside of our virtual classroom.

But Manjari Ma'am didn't let us linger in shock for long. 'To lift the mood,' she said with a smile, 'we're going to have a fun project. I need you to collect photos of every student, create a collage and post it on Instagram. The class with the most likes will win a prize.'

The change in energy was instant. 'That sounds cool!' Saurabh typed enthusiastically. 'Lessgooo!'

'Hell yeah!' I quickly typed. Soon, others joined in, too.

'Great! I'll send out the details soon,' Manjari Ma'am replied. 'Looking forward to seeing your creative collages!'

When we started planning the project, the disappointment just melted away. The task of making a photo collage became our new focus, and the excitement of working together on something fun brought us closer. It was a chance to turn our day around and create something enjoyable out of it.

This was not just a project; it was a way to bond and work together, and as we worked on it, the mood lightened and the sense of camaraderie grew stronger.

The Mystery of the Purple Saree

The collage project was in full swing. A group of five volunteers—Pavni, Saurabh, Mayur, Akinchan and I—had created a separate WhatsApp group to manage the task. I was responsible for collecting photos from ten students. It was a challenge, especially since I had never met these people in person and only had their numbers.

'Hey everyone,' I typed into the group chat, 'I'm collecting photos for the collage. Could you please send yours by today?'

Most people responded quickly. Messages flew back and forth, and the collage started to take shape. But as the hours ticked by, I noticed that photos from one student were still missing.

Determined to track this person down, I sent a message to the number: 'Hi! Can you please share your photo for the collage? Thanks!'

The reply came almost instantly: 'Hey Dev, give me a minute. I'm sending it to you now.'

A few moments later, a photo popped up on my screen. I stared at it, captivated. The girl in the picture was wearing a breathtaking purple saree. It was clear this was a special occasion—probably a farewell from her class 12th. Her curly hair framed her face beautifully, and her eyes were deep and mesmerizing. The saree added a touch of traditional grace, and her whole demeanour spoke of elegance and poise.

I was about to type a 'thank you' when I noticed a new message: 'Hi, I'm Avantika. Sorry for the delay. How's the collage coming up?'

'Hi, Avantika! The collage is coming together well. Thank you so much for sending your photo. It's beautiful!' I replied, feeling a strange but comforting connection through the screen.

As I looked at her photo again, I felt a strange emotion. The grace and warmth she exuded seemed almost unreal. Her picture gave a kind of real flavour to my rather mundane online existence.

'Are you ready to attend college in person?' I asked, in a feeble attempt to fill in the blank of our online presence with a connection to the reality that both of us missed.

'Definitely! It's strange starting this way, but I'm looking forward to meeting everyone in person someday,' Avantika responded.

Her words echoed my own feelings. Even though we hadn't met face-to-face, her photo and our brief conversation made the experience feel a bit more personal and real.

Sitting on the balcony on that rainy day in Goa, I smiled as I thought about how each photo and each conversation was a step towards building something meaningful. I felt bittersweet longing for the moments

I was missing and the connections I was just beginning to understand. It reminded me that while technology had brought us closer in some ways, it had also kept us apart. The journey was unusual, but it was full of unexpected beauty and connections.

As the writer Anaïs Nin once said, '*We do not see things as they are, we see them as we are.*'

The Defenders and the Unexpected Twist

Avantika was different. The only one from the science stream in our class of commerce students. And, naturally, that didn't go unnoticed.

One day, in our WhatsApp group, Saurabh, the joker, couldn't help himself.

'Science student in a commerce college? Lost on the way to IIT, Avantika?' he wrote, adding a line of laughing emojis.

I saw the message and waited. This was going to be interesting.

Avantika shot back almost instantaneously, 'Better lost and learning than stagnant in one place forever!' I could hear the sting in her comments, even from miles away.

Saurabh, never one to miss a beat, replied, 'Right, because balance sheets are sooo adventurous!'

But before I could chuckle, a new player entered the game. Manvit, a guy I hadn't even noticed before, suddenly chimed in.

'Chill, Saurabh,' he typed. 'It's not cool to judge someone for their choices. We're all here to learn, aren't we?'

Whoa. Where did that come from?

Saurabh, caught off-guard, quickly replied, 'Hey, man, just kidding around.'

But Manvit wasn't having it. 'Yeah, well, keep it friendly,' he shot back.

The group chat was click-clacking with reactions—thumbs-ups, laughing emojis, even some popcorn GIFs. I was riveted to my screen, waiting to see what would come next.

Avantika was the first one to break the tension. 'Thanks, Manvit, but I'm good.'

Manvit responded, 'I know. Just didn't like the vibe.'

And that was it. A straightforward exchange, yet it left me scratching my head. Did they know each other? Was this just random? The dude who was defending her like he was in some courtroom drama? It felt . . . unexpected.

In the days that followed, I noticed them chatting more. A comment here, a reply there. I kept telling myself I'd find the right moment to jump in, maybe even ask if they knew each other. But I never did. I kept watching from the sidelines, a spectator in my own story.

And maybe that was my biggest mistake.

Suddenly, my phone buzzed, and RKD's (Rahil) name flashed on the screen. I opened the message to find: 'Hey, I got into Christ!'

I stared, astonished. RKD, my best friend, known for his unusual crushes on women who were at least fifteen years older than him, was joining me at Christ.

With two people leaving, he had managed to get in. It felt like a sitcom moment: The guy who was always falling for teachers was finally getting his wish. I could already picture the next three years: Endless debates about who was 'hot' and who wasn't, punctuated by RKD's classic lines about 'mature' ladies.

Laughing at the absurdity, I thought, 'If this doesn't make for a wild ride, I don't know what will!'

At six in the evening, as I was down to the last few puffs of my cigarette, I was torn between diving into the mounting pile of assignments and losing myself in memories.

Just then, Manav called. 'Hey, let's step out. It's a beautiful evening. How about a break?'

Manav was a unique character. His thoughts were so original that he was the only person I've met who goes to bed at exactly 11 p.m., as if his life depended on it. A friend from my B-school days at IIM Goa, he's also a Christite, though a year ahead of me. A big-time procrastinator but he had the discipline of a monk—quite contradictory, isn't it?

The invitation felt like a lifeline. I grabbed my jacket and headed out. As I left the balcony where I'd been lost, deep in my thoughts, I realized how much had changed since those online days. Though life had moved on, the memories from that time still send jolts through my heart, bringing both smiles and tears. Sometimes, the past feels like a comforting friend, reminding me of how we've all grown.

Scooty Rides and Unexpected Encounters

I went out with Manav on his so-called *scooty*, which, to be honest, was barely holding itself together.

'Manav, I am telling you, if this scooty breaks down one more time, we're gonna have to start walking.'

'Ah, come on! It's not about the ride, it's about the adventure!' Manav replied, grinning from ear to ear.

Soon, I realized that I had forgotten my college ID and almost panicked. But then I remembered: senior privileges. I flashed my most charming smile at the guard *bhaiya* and said, *'Bhaiya, bas 5 minute mein aa raha hu.'* He waved us through with a knowing smile.

As we stopped for tea and a cigarette, Manav and I delved into our usual deep, philosophical conversation. It was mostly about how IIM Goa seemed like it was auditioning for the role of 'Worst Managed B-School' while still being one of the best in the country. I said, *'Yaar, iss college ka tagline,* "where learning never stops" *se change karke* "where learning never happens" *ho jana chahiye,'* and Manav burst out laughing.

Our conversation drifted from IIM Goa quirks to the universal truth about cigarettes: 'A cigarette is a temporary escape from reality, but also a reminder of your lack of control.' We shared a laugh about how, sometimes, a cigarette feels like the best friend who's always there for you—even if it's not the healthiest relationship.

To balance the ill effects of my smoking and to feed my passion, we went to play badminton. I was once quite good at badminton—at least, I told myself I was. The game was my escape, my means of feeling alive and competitive. But then cigarettes came creeping into my life; my footwork became less about finesse and more about fumbling with a smoke in one hand. It felt as if I'd exchanged my shuttlecock for a pack of 'cancer sticks', as my friends used to call them.

I noticed a girl standing by the badminton court. At first glance, she looked oddly familiar—curly hair, pink T-shirt, black trousers and pink shoes. *Is this déjà vu, or am I just seeing a ghost from the past*? I thought to myself.

She seemed to be waiting for her friends, and I couldn't help but wonder: *The girl is clearly obsessed with pink*.

I approached her and said, 'Excuse me, are you waiting to play? Want to join us?'

She turned around, and I froze for a second as I noticed her big, expressive eyes and her broad, gentle face. She reminded me so much of Avantika. Her curly hair framed her face in a way that added to her charm, bouncing with every movement as if it had a life of its own. There was something captivating about her—a quality that went beyond mere physical appearance.

She had a smile that could light up a room, and her presence felt like a breath of fresh air.

'Yes, I'd love to join,' she said with a bright smile. She introduced herself as Arushi, and we started our match. She was a fairly good player, and eventually, we won the game. Despite my footwork being somewhat rusty—the thought of those 'few too many' cigarettes—I did enjoy playing that game.

We talked casually after the match. Every word made her warm smile sparkle with delight in her eyes, and I appreciated the simplicity of being around her. It seemed like we shared much more.

It looked like old wine in a new glass. I couldn't help but recall that Avantika's dad had also been with Punjab National Bank. Arushi's resemblance to Avantika was uncanny—her big eyes, broad head and even her smile. It was as if the universe was serving me a familiar vintage under a different label.

We kept chatting and before she left, I gave her some friendly advice. 'Look, the secret to getting through college is simple: just act like you have it all together while secretly Googling everything. Works like a charm!'

Arushi laughed, 'I'll keep that in mind. So, basically, fake it till you make it?'

'Exactly!' I laughed. 'It's a timeless strategy. Works in college, and apparently, works in life, too.'

After exchanging our contact information, Arushi left the court with a grin and me looking around, staring at my mobile screen. A strange excitement mixed with uneasiness took over me. I kept scrolling through WhatsApp only to land on that message again:

'Can we be strangers again?' It had been five hours since I had received it.

A gnawing tugged at my heart, a returning sense of terror. I'd known the one who had just sent me that message for four years. Four years of sharing memories, late-night confessions of joy and misery and everything and nothing. Yet, this was the same person who wanted nothing at all now!

'Was it my fault? Did I miss a sign? Was there something I could have done differently?' My mind was in a loop of 'what ifs' and regrets.

I couldn't help but wonder, 'Should I say sorry? But what for? What did I even do? I had invested everything, every little bit of myself.'

I was lost in a whirlwind of thoughts when Manav interrupted and said, 'Let's go.'

'Everything okay?' he asked, realizing something was not okay with me.

I managed a weak smile. 'Yeah, just dealing with some stuff.'

He nodded, sensing that I wasn't ready to talk about it. 'All right, man. Let's get out of here. I need to head back to my room anyway.'

Walking back with Manav, I couldn't shake the feeling that the universe had a funny way of sending reminders of the past. Whether it was Arushi's resemblance to Avantika or the shared experiences that connected us all, life had a way of making old memories resurface in unexpected ways.

Manav, sensing my reflective mood, quipped, *'Yaar, jo bhi hai, itna* deep *mat soch.'*

And, of course, this is exactly why I sometimes have a grudge against people whose names start with 'M'.

I couldn't help but think: *Sharing your emotions with a guy is like trying to explain the plot of* Inception *to a three-year-old—confusing and messy, mostly leaving everyone frustrated. That's why every guy needs a female friend. They're the ones who can actually decode our emotional state and help us sort the mess without making us feel like we're just flailing around in the dark.*

We had just come back to our room—our 'cluster', to be precise. One of the few perks of doing an MBA at IIM Goa was getting to choose who lived next door or across the hall.

Being in the second year, we were supposed to have some privileges—or so they claimed. Our cluster was made up of four guys: Priyam, Abhay, Manav and I. Nothing particularly glamorous about it—just four survivors in this B-school jungle, where every day felt like an unscripted episode of a reality show that none of us had auditioned for.

I laughed in my mind. The cluster system was a mixed blessing. On one hand, we got to choose our neighbours, which meant we could avoid living next to the overzealous kids who were always ready to recite Porter's Five Forces at 3 a.m. On the other hand, we had . . . well, us.

Tonight was one of those nights when there wasn't much to do, aside from stressing about a case study due in less than twenty-four hours. Naturally, we finished off a bottle of Old Monk. 'Goa is a drinkers' paradise,'

I announced, raising the empty bottle as though it was the trophy I'd just claimed. 'Two hundred and fifty bucks for this magic potion? Forget ROI; we've got rum!'

Manav, lying on his bed, smiled. 'Forget the fees, man. The real ROI of an MBA in Goa is the affordable booze and sunsets.'

He looked at me with that you-know-the-one look, the one that meant, 'Give me something good.'

'So, what's next?' he asked, likely waiting for my genius plan.

I shrugged, 'Next? Just get placed. That's the plan. Keep whining until we get a job offer, decent enough to explain to our parents why we paid twenty lakh. I mean, I got in here with a solid 91.10 percentile. For what? Did all that just to be in this MBA circus where we're mastering the fine art of making PowerPoints look like strategic masterpieces.'

He nodded, 'Or, at least, hoping the placement office has enough *feni* to get us through the madness of Day Zero.'

I replied, 'Or, at least, hoping that the companies that come here don't ask too many questions beyond, "tell me about yourself", because we're all running out of creative answers for that one. Anyway, who has time for original thoughts when you have ChatGPT to copy-paste your way ahead?'

He chuckled. 'True. And let's be honest, we're all just here acting like we're picking up the secrets of management while, in reality, we're just learning how to survive on caffeine, cheap booze and instant ramen.'

We laughed, both of us knowing that this was the mantra of every MBA student on this campus.

At that moment, there was a knock on the door. I winced internally, already dreading the corporate smile I'd have to summon. Who could it be now? Another MBA soldier, most likely in need of some sort of an alliance or just a crash pad. I opened the door, prepared for the usual pleasantries, but was relaxed to see that it was Priyam.

I thought, 'Oh, it's him. Guy doesn't drink, doesn't smoke—sometimes I wonder, *yeh banda oxygen waste kyun kar raha hai?*'

'*Party chal rahi hai kya?*' Priyam asked enthusiastically, though it was clear he wasn't here for the booze.

Manav looked up, barely containing his laughter. '*Nahi yaar, mujra chal raha hai! Aaja* dance *karle!*' he said, playfully mocking the excitement of college parties.

Priyam, who was also in our cluster and a fellow Christite (yes, we had three of us in the same cluster; quite the coincidence), had a knack for bringing the most random energy into our otherwise mundane lives. Despite the fact that our batches were different and I joined Christ University just as Priyam was getting his graduation degree, it was clear that he was still the life of the cluster.

'*Wese bhi,* Dev *ko dekh ke toh lagta hai mujra hi chal raha hoga!*' Priyam mocked me.

I thought to myself, '*Yeh zinda kyun hai?*'

I turned to him and said, 'Bro, I graduated in 2023 and joined this jail—sorry, I mean MBA—in 2023.'

Despite the playful banter and his seemingly endless energy, Priyam's presence was a reminder that even in the chaos of MBA life, there were moments of camaraderie and absurdity that made it all worthwhile.

Eventually, we all crashed for the night, each of us going back to our rooms with a mix of useless gossip and half-hearted attempts at sleep. As I drifted off, I glanced at the clock—it was already 5:10 a.m.

But as soon as I closed my eyes, that message popped back into my mind. Although I was half drunk, I couldn't shake the thought of it.

'It takes the consent of two to build a relationship, but only one's decision to shatter it.' The quote echoed painfully in my mind, hitting me like a sledgehammer.

I set ten alarms to make sure I would wake up in time. It was an ambitious plan: 7:15, 7:20, 7:25 and so on. I thought that if I set enough alarms, I would possibly wake up. If nothing else, my room would be treated to a cacophony of blaring tones to usher in the morning—like it or not.

Having woken up at about 8:25 a.m., wallowing in the suitability of an unambiguous hangover, I hurried to brush my teeth and prepare myself for a lecture. I never understood why so many teachers were obsessed with classes at 9 a.m. I rushed to get ready and spotted Priyam lounging in the common area.

'Yaar, Priyam, iss prof. ko bol yaar, 9 baje kon lecture rakhta hai?' I complained.

As we both rushed through our morning routine, it was clear that in the world of MBA life, some things were just too absurd to make sense.

I was barely functioning, having dragged myself to class all hungover. As usual, we managed to claim the last seats in Paddy Sir's lecture.

Paddy Sir's lecture had a soothing quality to it, with his voice carrying a gentle rhythm that created a dangerously calming atmosphere. It felt as if his tone was designed to encourage relaxation rather than alertness, making it all too easy to doze off.

As we settled in, the first repeated question of the day came up, one I had heard in almost every lecture over the past twenty-two sessions.

'Did you all have breakfast? What was it?' asked Sir.

Priyam, even at 9:30 in the morning, was full of energy and, without fail, gave a response. 'Yes, Sir!' Full of energy, he said, 'It was aloo paratha!'

I looked at Priyam with appreciation for his spirit, yet with some surprise at how he could appear so alive, having had such little sleep and such seemingly inadequate food.

While Sir continued with his lecture in a calm manner, it was obvious that he was not a very exciting lecturer and was likely to make me sleepy rather than keep me awake.

Suddenly, my phone buzzed. It was a call from Mahesh Sir, a professor from Christ University. It had been over a year since we last spoke, so I was puzzled by the call. However, taking the call in the middle of Sir's lecture wasn't an option. I decided to wait until the lecture ended, planning to call Mahesh Sir back after the class.

The lecture dragged on, and I anxiously checked the clock. Finally, at 10:15, the lecture wrapped up, and I made a beeline for the exit. My mind was already set on having the same breakfast Priyam had enjoyed—something hearty to revive me from the morning's struggle.

I finally had my breakfast, and the remnants of my hangover were beginning to fade. As I settled into a more alert state, I remembered that I needed to call Mahesh Sir back.

When I dialled his number, he greeted me with his usual warmth. 'Good morning, Mr Dixit!'

I reciprocated the greeting with the same enthusiasm, 'Good morning, Sir!'

He asked how everything was going, to which I replied, 'It's good, Sir. Everything's going well.'

Mahesh Sir quickly got to the point. 'We're planning an alumni meet in January, and I wanted to see if you could schedule your plans around that. Your presence would be much appreciated.'

I smiled and assured him, 'Of course, Sir. I'll be there.'

After ending the call, I felt a sense of relief and satisfaction, knowing I had taken care of an important task.

I had only one lecture for the day, so I scurried back to my room for a much-needed six-hour nap, hoping to catch up on some lost sleep. As I was settling in, my phone buzzed with a text from Pavni.

'Are you planning to come?' she asked. Before I could reply to the text, my phone rang.

It was Pavni. 'Hey, did you get the call too?' she asked.

'Yep, I did. I guess we're the special ones now. I told him I'd be there—mostly because I want to show off how well I can pretend to be a responsible adult.'

'Definitely. I'm pretty sure Mahesh Sir sees us as some kind of "legendary alumni"—you know, the ones who survive on caffeine and good intentions.'

We both laughed, knowing that, in the end, our importance might be exaggerated, but, at least, we had a good story to tell.

After the call with Pavni, I lit up a cigarette and checked my phone. Opening WhatsApp, I saw the message still waiting for a reply—a glaring reminder of the emotional turmoil I had been trying to escape for the past day.

Each time I saw the message, it was like a persistent nudge, forcing me to confront the whirlwind of emotions I had been dodging.

With a heavy heart and tears threatening to spill out, I typed out my response: 'If being strangers is what you need to find your happiness, then I'll step back. I just want you to be at peace, even if it means losing a part of myself.'

I hit 'send' and looked at her name saved on my phone—Tam. I had always called her that, a tender nickname that felt like a secret between us, a small piece of affection that meant the world to me.

The cigarette I was smoking was calming, but only temporarily. It helped me a little but the chaos was relentless and wilful even during the calm.

With every puff, I started drifting closer to reminiscences of her, the times that felt more complicated, devoid of simplicity. 'I hope we never meet again,' I found myself mumbling with frustration.

Thinking of her as an elusive joy in life or as my second-worst mistake was what I intended. For me, the memories were too heavy to bear.

In the midst of all this reflection, I recalled having a bad hangover. It was also apparent that I needed a six-hour long snooze. However, my thoughts were telling a completely different story. My feelings and memories were entangled in a spiral. Escaping such a situation was nearly impossible for me. Suddenly, I felt an urge to approach the past moments instead of running away from them.

New Faces and Unseen Connections

With a deep breath, I exhaled. I was ready to reconnect the dots, to pick up where I had left and to understand the path that had led me here.

Thinking about it made me chuckle, especially when I remembered our online classes. Despite our best efforts to look engaged, the reality was far different. Our webcams were always on, creating the illusion of attentiveness, but our WhatsApp group was a flurry of jokes, memes and random chatter. The disparity between our polished Zoom appearances and our actual interest levels was contradictory.

One day, during a particularly monotonous lecture, I noticed a new face on the WebEx screen—a girl whom I'd never seen before in any of our previous classes. I thought to myself, 'Who's this? Did she just crash our class, or is she part of some secret club of elusive students?'

Maybe she was a latecomer. I wondered if she was there to occupy the final vacant spot left by two students who had left Christ, with Rahil filling one seat and this girl possibly the last one. Maybe she was the final piece in our virtual seating puzzle!

Our unofficial group chat was soon populated with questions like, 'Who is she?', and 'Has anyone seen her before?' Nobody knew, so I peered closer at the screen.

Without skipping a beat, I typed in the chat, 'I think her name is Tanishka.'

In the end, the lesson of the online class was not so much about the material of the course, but more about trying to remember who was who, even when the lectures started to fade into the background of our increasingly expanding digital social life.

I made some online friends, Pavni and Saurabh, who were like a breath of fresh air in my otherwise dull digital world. Pavni was always bubbling with ideas for extracurricular activities, dragging us into all sorts of virtual fests and events. Saurabh was our go-to guy for navigating Manjari Ma'am's tricky lectures— our half-hour crush who somehow made those boring sessions a bit more bearable.

There were times I wanted to join these fun activities with Avantika, but I never had the courage to say 'hi' or ask her to join. I kept thinking that she and Manvit must have some kind of chemistry, and I didn't want to be the awkward third wheel, the *'kabab mein haddi'*. So, I stayed in the background, imagining how different things could have been if I'd had the nerve to reach out.

A few days later, I realized that everyone seemed to be finding their own romantic connections. Pavni, with her usual flair, dropped the bombshell that she'd received a proposal. Saurabh and I were left staring at her on the G-Meet screen, our faces a perfect blend of shock and confusion.

Seriously? I thought, feeling a mix of envy and amusement. *Online love? How does that even work? Here I am, struggling to find the courage to say 'hi' to Avantika.*

Pavni mentioned she hadn't accepted the proposal yet, which only added to the whirlwind of emotions I was navigating. It felt like everyone was on a quest to find their soulmate or at least a hook-up buddy for the next three years, while I was still fumbling in the background. It was both funny and cringeworthy, seeing everyone else getting into relationships, while I was still trying to figure out how to talk to Avantika.

Birthday Surprises and Unspoken Wishes

Days turned into weeks, and the mix of online classes, assignments and incessant Google Meets began to settle into a pattern. To Pavni, Saurabh and me, virtual learning was more of a routine and less of an unconventional experience. These digital get-togethers turned into a source of comfort—allowing us to take our minds off everything academic, and laugh, joke around and enjoy each other's company.

During the dullness, I found it particularly interesting that Saurabh was also attempting to tackle the challenges of online dating. The plethora of proposals and attempts Saurabh made were, to say the least, quite depressing due to the fact that he had yet to find a matching partner. From a detached perspective, it was rather painful yet entertaining to watch Saurabh desperately searching for love.

The pages of the calendar flipped, and my birth month brought with it chilly winds and the vibrant colours of nature—October had arrived.

Like every typical night, on October 13, around 11:55 p.m., I lay tucked under my blanket, lazily scrolling through reels on my phone. Suddenly, a notification popped up on my screen: *'Jaldi se yeh meeting join kar!'* It was from Pavni. I sat up as the adrenaline and curiosity hit me. I did not waste a second, picked up my laptop and went to open it, my fingers falling all over the keyboard in anticipation. I joined the Google Meet as soon as the clock struck midnight and the atmosphere was electric. Pavni and Saurabh had organized a Google Meet celebration for my birthday, about ten to twelve classmates were already in the Meet, their faces framed on my screen, popping up one after the other. They had prepared a heart-warming video for me. The video had chronicled our history together, covering all the inside jokes we knew, and all the quirky things that had happened.

Others chimed in with their wishes too—laughing, joking and making the virtual room feel a little warmer. Despite all the noise and chatter, my eyes kept darting to the participants list, waiting for one particular name to appear.

Noticing my distraction, Pavni nudged me with a sly smile. 'You're waiting for her, aren't you?'

I shrugged, trying to play it cool. 'Maybe . . .'

Saurabh chuckled and said, 'Do you want me to give Avantika a call?'

Before I could respond, Pavni, ever the bold and proactive friend, interjected. 'Don't even think about it,' she said with a hint of a smile. 'If you ask, she might never show up.'

Pavni grabbed her phone with a determined look. 'Don't worry, I'll handle this,' she declared, scrolling through her contacts. 'If anyone can convince her, it's me.'

She dialled Avantika's number, glancing over at me with a wink. 'Let's see if she picks up,' she whispered, as I held my breath, waiting to see if she'd join the celebration.

Pavni's call rang only for a moment before Avantika picked up. I watched her closely, unable to hear Avantika's voice on the other end, but I could see Pavni; her mic was unmuted.

'Hey, Avantika! It's Dev's birthday today,' she said, grinning wide enough to stretch across the screen. 'We've set up a Google Meet to celebrate. Do you want to join us?'

I sat there, my eyes fixed on Pavni's face, trying to read every little reaction. I had no idea what Avantika was saying, but I was hanging on to every second, my mind racing with the possibilities. I hadn't ever talked to her properly, hadn't even seen her beyond her profile picture. Still, there was this strange pull, a flutter of hope that she might just say yes.

Pavni hung up the call, flashing a quick, triumphant smile in my direction. My heart was racing, my palms suddenly a bit sweaty. She was coming. Avantika was actually joining the call.

I felt a rush of happiness, an involuntary grin stretching across my face. My heart skipped a beat. I didn't know why it mattered so much or why I was this excited, but it did. I couldn't shake the feeling that maybe, just maybe, something momentous might happen.

My heart raced as a notice flashed on the screen. It read 'Avantika Sharma has joined the call.' There she was, right in front of me, visible in real-time.

'Happy Birthday, Dev!' she said with a warm smile.

'Thank you,' I muttered, trying to sound nonchalant, as a blast of heat rushed over my face. I thought I covered it up well, but the rigged awkwardness of my tone must have given it away.

The teasing began almost immediately. Akinchan was grinning from ear to ear and blurted out, *'Bhai ka din ban gaya!'* Everyone burst into fits of laughter, throwing in goofy remarks.

Avantika looked around, a bit puzzled, trying to figure out what was going on. She smiled politely, but it was clear she had no idea why everyone seemed so delighted, why all eyes were darting between her and me. The whole call knew—or thought they knew—about my so-called 'crush'. Maybe it was just an infatuation, but whatever it was, it had become the worst-kept secret among my friends.

As the clock ticked towards 1 a.m., the Google Meet session continued with some fun chat. Chirag, one of our classmates, even got in on the action, mimicking Monika Ma'am's distinctive tone as we pretended to roast her in good humour. The room filled with laughter as everyone enjoyed the light-hearted moment.

Soon after, everyone began to leave as well, each wishing me a happy birthday once more before exiting the call.

Eventually, the list of attendees reduced to just a few. Avantika was still there, but I couldn't muster the courage to make eye contact. I focused on the quiet screen, savouring the birthday cheer as everyone finally signed off, leaving me alone with the echoes of the night's celebration.

After the meeting ended, I picked up my phone and headed to bed. I glanced at the notifications. The BCOM-B Unofficial group chat was overflowing with 'Happy Birthday, Dev' messages. It seemed like every member had chimed in, adding their own touch to the birthday wishes.

Scrolling through WhatsApp, I saw countless birthday messages from school friends, many of which seemed like mere continuations of previous conversations, almost as if they were just following the trend of birthday greetings. It felt like a routine yearly exchange, with everyone sending their obligatory wishes.

Among the notifications, I noticed one from an unknown number. Curiosity piqued, I opened the chat to find a birthday wish from someone I didn't recognize.

A mix of confusion and intrigue washed over me. *Who could this be?* I wondered, trying to figure out the mystery behind the anonymous birthday wish.

I replied with a simple 'thank you.'

I then typed out another message: 'Do we know each other?'

Suddenly, a reply popped up. 'No, we don't know each other,' came the response. 'Hi, I'm Tanishka.'

I remembered her as the last person to join our class—the one who had appeared out of nowhere, in our boring WebEx meeting.

We had a brief conversation about how the classes were evolving and how she was new to such a set-up, especially as she joined in late.

'Anyway, I heard that the Karnataka government approved hybrid learning, so we'll be there in December,' I said.

She replied, 'Yeah, I've heard that too. Online classes feel more like a background soundtrack while we scroll through memes and pretend to be engaged.'

I smiled and thought, 'Yeah, that's pretty much what I do too.'

I replied, 'Yeah, you're right.'

Our conversation continued briefly about college assignments, but soon we wrapped up. I said, 'Same here, Tanishka. It was really nice talking with you. Let's keep in touch and help each other out.'

We wrapped up the conversation with a friendly 'bye!' and a wave emoji.

I suddenly noticed that the cigarette was almost gone, just the bud remained between my fingers.

It was that iconic conversation that dragged me into a storm I never saw coming. A storm that still raged inside me, pulling me apart, leaving me stranded somewhere between what was and what could have been. *'If only that birthday wish had never come . . . if I had never opened that message,'* I murmured to myself, as if wishing could undo the past.

But regret never changes the past; it only makes the present harder to bear. And in that moment, all I wanted was to forget . . . to un-feel. But how do you un-feel something that still feels so deeply?

I stared at the fading daylight through the window, feeling the pull of the night ahead. The noise of the world seemed far away, and I was alone again with my thoughts.

Suddenly, I heard the all-too-familiar ding from my phone—the Microsoft Outlook notification that every MBA student has come to despise. Honestly, who actually likes that sound? It's like they designed it specifically to disturb whatever tiny shred of calm we have left.

I picked up my phone, squinting through the headache, and saw an email: *Pre-Placement Talk scheduled at 2 p.m. for students without classes today*. Fantastic. An invitation to sit in a room full of excessively excited recruiters, nodding as if we were all in one, and acting like the 'ideal candidate' was exactly what I needed. A list of pupils who were 'fortunate' enough to be selected for this enjoyable occasion was included in the email.

With a sigh, I clicked on the Excel file. I typed 'Dev' in the search bar. No one else on this campus has the audacity to share this name with me. And, of course, there it was—highlighted in bright yellow like some kind of prize I'd won. Fantastic.

I groaned. 'I don't want to go. I just want to sleep.' But no, they just had to drag us out for these pre-placement talks, making us parade around in Western business formals with clean-shaven faces. Seriously, who even made that a rule? The thought of it made me grumble, 'Beard is the jewellery of men!'

Two hours to go.

'Man, I'm hungover . . . I can't deal with one more thing today. Paddy Sir's class was enough punishment.'

I flopped back down onto my bed, pulling the blanket over my head like it could shield me from reality. Maybe if I stayed still long enough, the world would forget I existed for just a bit longer.

Man, as much as I wanted to just bury myself under the blanket and pretend this day didn't exist, the thought of paying a fine—or worse, being debarred from the placement cycle—was enough to make me move.

My dad had taken a loan just to get me here, to see me 'placed' in some shiny job with a hefty paycheck. Skipping wasn't an option.

I dragged myself out of bed and dug through the chaos that was my wardrobe. After some digging, I found a crisp white shirt that looked presentable and a pair of trousers. Then I found my black blazer that I hoped could still pass as 'Western business formal'.

Then came the part that I dreaded most—my beard. I went to the washroom and stared at my reflection in the mirror, admiring my beard . . . The beard looked good, like it always did, adding a bit of edge to my face. It was full and perfectly shaped—the kind of beard that made you look like a rugged adventurer in a suit, rather than someone who just crawled out of bed. 'Beard is the jewellery for men,' I grumbled again, trying to convince myself I could get away with just trimming it. But no, clean-shaven was the rule. With a sigh, I grabbed the razor and went to work, shaving off my dignity with every stroke. The hangover was bad enough; now I had to face the world barefaced too?

With my face feeling unnervingly smooth and the hangover still showing in my eyes, I trudged towards the auditorium. The sun seemed a little too bright, the world a little too loud. By the time I got there, a line had already formed, almost coiling down the entire hallway like some unending line of people waiting for a new iPhone launch. I stood in line, choking back a wince every time someone laughed or spoke a bit too loudly.

Eventually, I managed to find a seat at the back. Not the best location, but at least I wouldn't have to pretend to be excited from the front row. Two individuals took the stage, fiddling nervously with the mic as if it was a bomb about to go off. Finally, it worked, and one of them leaned in with an ear-to-ear grin and an overly enthusiastic voice: 'Good afternoon, students!'

I rolled my eyes and muttered, 'Good afternoon, my ass . . .' Their cheery Alaska accents vibrated through the speakers, and as they continued with their naive cheer, my temple throbbed. As the bespectacled chap droned on about 'opportunity' and 'career growth', my eyelids grew heavier with every syllable.

The one with the tight bun and the unyielding frown carried on: 'Good morning. Let me welcome you to this fabulous, pre-placement talk by Globex Corporation. We are an international player in digital transformation, and innovation and excellence are something we embrace in everything we do.'

Great! Now I am really on my way to boredom.

She continued, adding, 'Globex Corporation is one of a select group within the Top 50 Employers

in the world, with a diverse portfolio, including
AI technologies and machine-learning capabilities,
through cutting-edge FinTech solutions. We take pride
in our colourful work culture, the importance we place
on employee development and the spirit of innovation.'

She added, 'Your network and your interactions
can shape your career trajectory.'

Networking? My brain scoffed. In this state, I was
more likely to network with a pillow than with a
potential employer. I leaned further into the chair and
quietly begged my clock for speed.

A headache grew from every bullet point they
listed. She was back again: 'Very competitive salary
package, very good benefits and continuous learning—
the experience at Globex is more about being partners
than employees, in our quest to become great.'

An hour later: 'Now, we'd like to take any questions
from the audience.'

Whatever you do, just don't ask anything, I silently
prayed as I could feel that throbbing pain building
again in my head. All I wanted was to lie back in bed,
curl up from this hangover and sleep forever.

Of course, there had to be the one sucker trying out.
A hand shot up almost immediately—from the front
row, a guy with glasses perched on his nose, looking
like he'd been waiting all his life for this moment.

'Yes, you,' the woman smiled, pointing him out.

'Thank you for that presentation. Can you please
tell us how Amtronix intends to integrate ESG principles
into its core corporate model and earn profitability in

emerging markets?' His voice boomed with the kind of enthusiasm that made me want to toss my chair at him.

I grimaced inwardly. That made me groan. ESG? Well, could you just kind of spoil it for the rest of us? But that was only the beginning. One by one, hands began bobbing up like thistles across the auditorium. There were a thousand questions, ranging from precise inquiries about market strategies to the general vision of the company.

Each of these questions felt like torture; time seemed to have slowed down, but my headache worsened.

Finally, the woman in the front said, 'Thank you for all of your wonderful questions. We hope we've given you some clarity on who we are and what we stand for. We look forward to engaging with you again throughout the rest of the recruitment process.'

A mild flutter of applause arose and, at that time, I was actually getting up half in haste to run toward the door. I managed to navigate my way through the crowd with all the talking around me before I finally found the exit.

Dashing into my room, I threw myself on my bed without bothering to change, embracing the comfort of the softest, most pillowy surface imaginable. Thank heavens, the headache was a notch less terrifying by now, in a world so much softer. I let out a long, drained-out sigh, covered myself with the blanket and surrendered to the comforting embrace of sleep.

Peace at last. Sleep was the only thing I needed, for now.

Echoes of What Could Have Been

I woke up at 8 p.m., my stomach growling, as I suddenly remembered I hadn't eaten since the morning's aloo paratha, before which I couldn't even remember what I ate. Drowsily, I changed out of the dreadful Western business formals—free at last—and rushed to the canteen.

When I reached there, the mouth-watering smell of chicken lal jhol engulfed me instantly. I felt my mouth water; there was a long queue of juniors waiting patiently, but I was not concerned. It was my right; after all, seniors have privileges, I told myself as I cut through. Some gave me looks, but I shrugged it off.

With a plate in hand, I said to the guy at the counter, *'Bhaiya, jitna de sakte ho do, bahut bhook lagi hai.'* He smiled knowingly and scooped a good helping of chicken onto my plate. I helped myself with three or four scoops of rice and moved towards an empty table.

I put my earphones on, ready to drown the day with some music. I launched Spotify, and the first song that came on was by Anuv Jain, *'Jo Tum Mere Ho.'* The tune softly melted through my ears as the lyrics went by, *'Pooche yeh tu ki tujhe mein main kya dekhta hoon, jab chaaron taraf aaj kitne hi saare nazaare hain.'*

The words crashed upon me like a tidal wave, and before I knew it, I was opening WhatsApp. My heart sank as I saw the notification—a message from Tam, the person who'd turned my world upside down just days ago. She had replied two hours ago.

'Live your life; don't get stuck on me.

'I'm removing you from Instagram and Snapchat. If you ever need anything, just let me know. I'll always be here for you.

'Goodbye and good luck with your placement.'

As I read her words, the ache in my chest deepened. The realization that she was now removing me from her digital world felt like a cold, sharp knife twisting in my heart. Despite being just a friend from her perspective, she was my one-sided love. For me, our bond meant everything—I never wanted a relationship from her, only a connection that I hoped would last forever. The memories of our friendship came flooding back—how she used to share everything with me, from the dress she wore to every little detail of her day. The gossip about Christ, the inside jokes and the bond we had, the person I confided in, the one who made my days brighter.

She was the person who taught me to love someone in moderation, to not be a fool by wasting emotions on someone who doesn't care.

Now, seeing her remove me from her life felt like erasing a part of my own soul. The depth of my feelings, once filled with hope and warmth, now lay in ruins.

I read the words again, and they felt like a punch to the gut. I could almost hear her voice saying it, soft but firm, trying to be kind yet distant. It was as if she was telling me to let go, to move on, but I wasn't ready to. Not yet. *How could she just . . .?*

My chest tightened, and for a moment, I felt breathless. My hands trembled slightly as I put the phone down. The music continued to play, the lyrics weaving into the moment, making it harder to hold back. I felt a sting in my eyes, and before I could stop it, a tear slipped down my cheek. I wiped it away quickly, glancing around to make sure no one noticed. But the canteen was too busy; no one was looking.

I closed my eyes, letting the music and the warmth of the chicken in my mouth offer some small comfort. *How do you un-feel something that still feels so real?*

I sat there, alone at the empty table, letting the weight of it all wash over me. The words she had typed felt like a finality I wasn't ready for, and yet, I knew I had to face it somehow . . . even if it broke me a little more with every passing moment.

I had been craving the chicken lal jhol all day, my stomach growling in anticipation. The rich, spicy flavours should have been a welcome relief from the haze of my hangover and the emotional storm I was in. But, as I took my first few bites, I realized that even this comfort food couldn't soothe me. After only a few spoonfuls, my appetite disappeared. I felt a peculiar heaviness, as if my heart was too full to appreciate the food in front of me.

The music on Spotify continued to play softly in the background, and the next song was *'Besar Rahee Sharabein, Besabar Ye Dil Jo Mera.'* The lyrics seemed to speak directly to the turmoil inside me: *'Besar rahi sharaabein, besabar ye dil jo mera, bewaqoof tha tere bina, beqaraar si thi raatein, beshumaar teri yaadein.'*

It was as if Spotify had taken my side during this heartbreak, capturing every feeling and regret within itself with such a voice that, at one point, generated a buzz in my heart. The words filled me completely and sharpened the pain in my heart. Every note reverberated through me; it played a melancholic underscore to my sorrow.

I finished dinner and went back to my room. All I wanted was to escape the circle of chaos and clutter that had been disturbing me throughout the day. The night air felt brisk and soothing as I walked along, a perfect contrast to the confusion in my mind.

I entered my room, locked the door and flopped down on the bed. The bed comforted me as peace and quiet engulfed me.

I lit my cigarette and let the smoke wrap around me as I tried to escape. I took a huge breath and opened Instagram to see if she genuinely removed me. I hit the search button and got to see that Tanishka's name came up with the recent searches. My heart started racing as I tapped on it.

The profile loaded; my eye fell on the blue 'Follow' button. It continued, saying below that, 'Followed by Pavni Arora and 71 others'. My gut shrank—it appeared as if the connections were still there; I felt rather miserable.

I quickly switched to Snapchat and prayed for some light. She was the first one on my list, but the streak was gone. Best friend status remained, however. Frayed connections but not completely torn apart—a bittersweet reminder of everything that once was.

The cigarette burned slowly between my fingers, the smoke curling up like the remnants of what we once had. I watched as the ember glowed faintly, a dying reminder of the warmth that once existed between us. Now, just like this cigarette, that warmth was fading into ash.

I opened WhatsApp again, her chat still sitting there at the top, mocking me with its silence; I stared at the message, feeling anger simmer beneath the surface. Her words, *'Live your life; don't get stuck on me,'* echoed in my mind. My fingers flew across the screen as I typed out what I truly wanted to say.

'So, you did it again, huh? Walked away as if I was nothing, like I didn't exist.' The promise she made— 'I won't leave you again'—was broken again. 'Does your "goodbye" make it easier for me to forget, or does it just help you sleep better at night?'

I stopped, my thumb hovering over the 'send' button.

But I knew she wouldn't care. She hadn't cared when she left before, when she replaced me so easily. She wouldn't care now. I could send a thousand messages, and it wouldn't change a thing.

I deleted the message, one letter at a time, until the screen was blank and empty again. Just like me . . .

A deep breath to calm the storm inside me failed this time, as the pain was too damn real, too raw. Big fat droplets threatened me again, and this time, I didn't fight them. They streamed down my cheeks, each drop a silent testimony to my lost love, to the promises that were nothing now.

'Why me?' I whispered into nothingness. 'Why is it always me who gets hurt?' My voice broke, and I felt my chest tighten, gasping for breath. I had given it my all, everything that I possessed, every piece of my being into this friendship, into this love. But was this it? Is this all I get in return? Is it really my destiny to be the one who gets left behind—the one who put too much effort and feelings into it, and loved too deeply?

Attachment is a weird feeling, quietly creeping into the cracks of being and becoming a part of who you are. But when it breaks, it snaps. It takes shards from you right along with it, leaving you hollow, empty, incomplete.

I stamped out my cigarette in the ashtray, wiped away my tears and thought about how it seemed like a cruel joke in the face of my anguish. *'You can't force someone to love you when they don't want to,'* I whispered to myself, trying to make sense of it all. Why do people forget those who once mattered to them when new faces come into their lives?

I couldn't help but wonder if this was just the way things were meant to be—some people love hard, and some leave easily.

As the silence settled, my mind drifted back to a different time, a different moment—back to 2020. Life then was a blend of hopeful beginnings and earnest efforts. Tanishka, Avantika and I were a TriPort, navigating the complexities of CIA assignments and college life.

Our bond was a source of strength and comfort; they were the bread and butter of my journey, the constant support that helped me push through challenges. Together, we tackled every obstacle, laughed at every mishap and celebrated each small victory.

Now, as I reflected on those days, I realized how pivotal two people had been in shaping my journey. Their impact hit me hard. Avantika had taught me a painful lesson about love's darker side. Her betrayal was simply more than grief; it was a stark reminder that love can be a ruse for manipulation. She didn't simply leave; instead, she betrayed my confidence and demonstrated to me how love can be used to manipulate and deceive.

Tanishka, on the other hand, had been my rock.

She showed me how to love in moderation and perspective. When Avantika's betrayal left me in pieces, Tanishka was the one who held me together. She dried my tears and helped me see that life is bigger than one person's hurt. Her support was my lifeline, guiding me through the darkest times.

As I grappled with the weight of these lessons, I couldn't help but wonder: How could someone who seemed so genuine turn out to be so cruel?

As I sat there, I couldn't help but think: *If only I had never met Avantika. If only I had never let myself get lulled into the lullaby of her love. If only I had never been there in that photo collage, her purple saree signifying more than I might ever know about love.*

Had I never let her into my world, had I never allowed myself to get entangled in her slippery web of manipulation, then maybe Tanishka and I could have continued on a different path. Possibly, things could have been better, less complicated, less painful.

Now these are thoughts, regretful trains from a bygone past I can never recover. It still hurts deeply, mingling with the pain of what things might have been walking on with one foot in front of the other, I am haunted by the ghosts of possibilities, a tremendous burden that won't let go.

I forced myself to go back to those memories, the ones that I try to forget. I kept thinking: *What if Pavni had not called Avantika on my birthday?* That night was beautiful, one of the best birthdays—clouded years later by doubt and regret.

I still resent Pavni for that call. What seemed innocuous at the time turned into a tragedy. Whereas it seemed like a perfect celebration, it ended up being a precursor to regret. In 2024, as I thought about the connections that came and went, I thought how exceedingly ironic—I ended up reaching out to two girls who one after the other left me behind.

That night of apparent joy reminds me of how life can sometimes take one of the most cherished moments and sow the seeds of future disturbance.

With a sigh of anger, I said, 'Ah Avantika . . . it makes me feel bad that I still think of her.' The sheer mention of her name sent a ripple of anger and regret through me. I tried forcing away the thoughts that filled my mind, but I couldn't help thinking back to her and what had happened.

When Flirting Turns to Feelings

I still remember it was 18 October, just four days after my birthday. That night, we chatted endlessly—the kind of night I'd thought was special, only to realize later it was the start of something I would one day regret. It was the night before our last midterm, the dreaded accounts exam. Of course, with the exam being online, hardly anyone was taking it seriously. Everyone in the group had made plans to cheat—because, well, who actually studies for an online exam?

That's when I got a message from Avantika, sliding into my DMs with a grin I could almost see through the screen. 'So . . . what's the cheat code for tomorrow? Need a road map!' It made me laugh out loud. I replied with a few ideas, and we went back and forth, building a little plan that was more a joke than a real strategy.

After the exam, she sent me a quick 'thanks!' and, somehow, that tiny word sparked a conversation that didn't stop. We started talking about everything—life, college, her recent move. I asked, 'So, where are you from in Rajasthan?' She surprised me by saying, 'Oh, I've lived in a bunch of places too—my dad's with Punjab National Bank, so we move around a lot.'

It caught me off guard, and I couldn't help but smile. 'No way, my dad also works at SBI!' I replied. And just like that, it felt like some cosmic signal that we were meant to cross paths. There were so many coincidences, so many things that seemed to connect us. The coincidence seemed almost too perfect, as if some invisible thread was pulling us closer.

We started chatting around 8 p.m., and before I knew it, the clock read 4 a.m. The conversation flowed like water, moving from casual banter to deeper, more personal territory. At some point, I found myself typing, 'So, are you dating anyone?'

She replied, 'No, I'm single.'

I couldn't help but tease her, 'What about Manvit? He always seemed like your knight in shining armour when Saurabh teased you on the ground.'

She laughed, 'Oh, Manvit? No, no. He did propose, but I friend-zoned him.'

I chuckled. 'Poor guy,' I said.

Then, she turned the tables, 'And what about you? Are you single?'

I couldn't resist adding a playful comment, 'Yeah, I know I'm handsome—guess I'm just a limited edition, not everyone's lucky enough to get one.'

She laughed, and I decided to keep the banter going. 'So, have you dated before?' I asked.

She hesitated for a second and then said, 'Yeah, there was this guy, a family friend . . .'

We laughed, but behind the jokes, something was brewing. The night was turning into something much more than just a random chat.

Then she suddenly asked, *'Koi pasand aaya Christ mein?'*

I stared at the screen for a moment, wondering if I should be upfront or just tease her a little. I decided to drop a hint instead.

So, I typed, 'Well, there *might* be this one girl . . . she's got a thing for purple sarees. Makes quite an impression, you know?'

A few seconds later, the typing indicator appeared, and then her message popped up: 'Purple sarees? That's oddly specific.'

I replied, 'Yeah, and she has this weird talent for keeping me awake till 4 a.m., talking about . . . well, basically everything.'

She replied, *'Chalo*, then you go to sleep, and I will, too. It was nice talking to you.'

I stared at her message, a twinge of regret hitting me. *Yaar, faltu ka bol diya,* I thought, over-analysing every word I'd just typed. I quickly turned off my data and decided to sleep it off.

When I woke up around 9 a.m., I checked my notifications. There it was—her message: 'Can we be friends *abhi ke liye?* When we meet physically, we'll see how things go. You have nice eyes, you know . . . And maybe, I might have had a small crush on you too.'

I stared at the screen, my heart doing somersaults. *A crush on me?* I read the message again, just to be sure. Suddenly, all my regrets from the night before felt a little less heavy.

Nice eyes? A smile crept onto my face, and suddenly, I was wide awake.

I jumped out of bed and rushed to the mirror. I stared at my reflection, leaning in closer, squinting a little, checking my eyes from every possible angle. '*Nice eyes, huh?*' I mumbled to myself, half-smiling.

I turned my head left, then right, even tried the classic Bollywood 'intense look' for good measure. 'Maybe she's onto something,' I chuckled

I grinned at my reflection and thought, 'Handsome *toh tu hai, yaar . . . ab* validation *toh mil chuki hai, aur kitni chahiye?*' I puffed up my chest a little, still admiring my own reflection.

'*Lagta toh hu main SRK jaisa, bas . . .*' I mumbled with a grin, still staring at the mirror.

I checked my phone and, after some hesitation, answered: 'Friends for now sounds great. Let's see where it goes when we meet in person. And thank you . . . That's a lovely compliment.'

Having calmed down a little, I entered the online class with a measly smile, with her words still lingering in my mind.

We talked about everything, day and night, like an unvoiced urgency to discover each other's secrets. Late-night chats turned to early-morning confessions, and with each message, I felt myself coming closer to her. The very beep of her messages would make my heart beat fast and give me butterflies. Very soon, her name became an excuse for my late nights, random smiles and a hundred checks on my phone.

A day or two later, Avantika and I were quite engrossed in a Zoom call when she nonchalantly said:

'I'd love for you to meet one of my friends. She's really great, and I think you two would hit it off.'

Interesting, I thought. 'Well, why not? Who's this friend of yours?' My curiosity piqued.

Avantika smiled as she arranged for her friend to join the call through text. A while later, a friendly face popped into view and said, 'Hi! I'm Tanishka,' with a wide smile.

I was greeted with silence for a moment. 'That's Tanishka?' I whispered as I racked my brain searching for our last conversations.

'That's me!' she said with a laugh.

I hadn't spoken to Tanishka for anything longer than five minutes on my birthday, but I already had a vague idea of her. But as the conversation progressed, it became clear that Tanishka and Avantika had a great friendship. They joked and chatted with ease, and I found myself enjoying the dynamic they shared.

It was clear that she was an important part of Avantika's life, and as we continued to chat, it became apparent that our circle of friends was expanding in the most unexpected and delightful ways.

As I looked back on it all, it hit me: two girls are like Oscar-winning actors—'You're my best friend!' to each other's faces, but the second they turn around it's all gossip and drama.

By December, as the Karnataka government allowed colleges to resume classes in hybrid mode, Avantika and I had grown quite close. It was quite a different situation compared to the acquaintances we once were. As for Tanishka, our connection remained on the peripherals, or superficial, so to speak. We were never truly close. Rather than forming a genuine bond, our interactions were more about navigating the complexities of our situation.

To be honest, I now understand how little our friendship was worth. Genuinely, it seemed Avantika had never wanted Tanishka and me to be close; perhaps, she viewed Tanishka as competition and didn't like our growing bond. Tanishka was always playing the mediator whenever Avantika and I had a falling-out, for what it was worth. Still, it was very palpable that her loyalties lay more with Avantika than me. Our camaraderie, reflective of hindsight, seemed more a mode of formality than a real friendship.

In a strange motley of shifting dynamics, the month of December came to represent the start of a new chapter. The notion of starting offline classes felt like an opportunity for a fresh start.

As the general saying goes, 'Sometimes the people you think are closest to you are the ones who are just good at pretending.'

A smile escaped my lips as I reminisced, rummaging through my bag for my Old Monk bottle. I liked to call it my personal time machine—a student-*y* drink if there ever was one: convenient, cheap and always around to ease your mind, even if it meant you would wake up nursing a huge hangover.

I finally picked up my phone and tapped on the college app. If there were an award for the most inconveniently timed reminders, this app would take home the trophy. 'Great, another lecture while nursing a hangover,' I muttered.

I poured myself a drink, then another and finally a third, preparing for a night of introspection and reckoning. As the alcohol started to do its job, I turned on the speaker and let Anuv Jain's songs fill the room. His melodies, with their haunting beauty, seemed to echo my own feelings of reflection and regret.

The reality of seeing someone for who they truly were—especially when they had been the centre of your universe—was a hard lesson learned. Making someone too important, allowing them to become your sun while you merely revolved around them, had been a mistake I'd learned the hard way.

The night was full of mixed emotions, and I knew a wild ride awaited me.

The flashbacks were just beginning, and I was sure the night would be anything but ordinary.

A Sweet December in Bengaluru

December came, and with it, my big move to Bengaluru. Ah, Bengaluru—this city has one of the best kinds of weather I've ever felt. It has one of the most consistently pretty skies, a cool breeze almost all around the year and a warm sun that feels nourishing as it hits the skin in the morning. In every sense, it felt like a fresh start. I had found a PG near Koramangala, on one of those lanes where the smell of coffee mingles with the overdrive on the road. There was something in the air that made it feel different—as if I was stepping into a new life, one that was bigger and more complicated.

But this wasn't just about the city—it was about college. When I finally stepped into campus, it hit me. This wasn't the Karan Johar movie kind of college with scenic lawns and endless hangouts. No, this was different.

Here, the most crucial accessory wasn't your phone or a pair of cool sunglasses, rather it was your ID card. Lose that, and you'd be treated like a criminal. And the dress code? Never mind casual—formal was the law of the land. Tucked-in shirts, polished shoes, perfectly knotted ties. Christ, if anything, had this weirdly articulate way of making sure you remember that here, things weren't just serious, they were *professional*. Every morning felt like you were dressing up for a board meeting rather than a lecture.

Walking through the gates, I saw my classmates in real life for the first time—faces I had only seen on WebEx, where they were just tiny squares on a screen. In person, everything was different. The atmosphere had a quiet intensity to it. Everyone was focused, driven. It was like the entire environment pushed you to do more, to be better.

There was a climate of excitement—students were enthusiastic, even borderline obsessed with participation, be it in class or the interminable events that proliferated our daily lives. It wasn't just about academics, but about being the best version of you in every way. I felt it—the urge to succeed, to stretch the limits and to keep up with the pace of those around me.

Christ was something wholly different—unique by all means. This wasn't just a college; it was a place of proving ground, a place where you felt the weight of expectation with every foot forward. But that pressure wasn't suffocating; it was challenging, an invitation to exceed the ordinary. And I was ready for it.

The excitement of sitting through classes, in person, was already bubbling inside me, but tomorrow was going to be something else—Avantika was coming. And so was Tanishka. I hadn't met either of them since we all got caught up in the web of online classes, and the prospect of finally getting to know them in person added one more level of tingling anticipation. It was no longer just about resuming offline classes—it felt like we were in a new stage of life, where each silent word and momentary smile held significance.

The Calm before the Storm

Before their arrival, I met a couple of classmates I had grown to share a good bond over the months—Pavni and Saurabh. There was something comforting about them. We'd talked a lot during our WebEx sessions, and now, in person, it was even easier to slip into conversation. We exchanged pleasantries, laughed about how awkward those tiny video windows had been, and it felt good. As if we'd been there before, only now, it was real.

But the real moment, the one that made my heart race, was seeing Avantika.

The next day, I was standing by the entrance to the campus, casually talking to Pavni and Saurabh when I spotted her. Avantika was getting out of the car with her parents. A pink top and black jeans—very simple, but very much her. Soft waves cascaded down her long hair, but what left me in awe were her eyes.

Her parents had dropped her off and somehow I found myself walking toward them with greeting words. Her mom greeted me warmly, and her dad gave me a firm handshake. 'What's up? Ready for this new chapter?' they queried. I nodded while exchanging some small talk, but my mind was elsewhere. All I could think about was Avantika: How she looked, how she held herself. It felt like one big perfect moment, as if every piece of the puzzle was falling into the right place.

Everything felt so good. So, so right.

I extended my hand to Avantika and as she smiled back at me, everything else was set to fade away for a second.

We decided to go to lovely Block 4, the canteen, where the aroma of the fried snacks and coffee scent lingered in the air. It was one of Christ's main hangout spots—nice by no means, but just perfect for a catch-up. Time went by too quickly and, soon, we were at our teasing game as always.

Amidst laughter, Avantika's phone rang. It was Tanishka, and with a quick 'she's here', we both got up and walked toward the gate to welcome her. And once Tanishka caught sight of Avantika, it was a cosmic-scale greeting scene straight out of a Bollywood film minus the music in the background. They ran toward one another like two sisters who hadn't met in a millennium, hugging each other so tightly that one might think they'd found each other by wearing invisible shoes.

'*Arre, chhod bhi do!*' I laughed, watching their never-ending hug that could probably last another millennium.

Finally, they pulled apart. Tanishka turned to me with a polite smile and offered a quick, formal handshake. No warmth, no real connection—just a clear sign that our bond had never really grown. We were still just . . . there, orbiting around Avantika.

After that, I couldn't help but ask, 'So, where are you guys staying?'

Avantika replied 'We're in a PG in Koramangala too!' and they were sharing a room together.

I tried to keep my tone casual, but inside, I was buzzing with excitement. 'I live there, too,' I responded. The idea of us being so close to each other in the same part of this fringy city turned me on in implicit ways of joy: not really because of the distance, but because it felt like lives were sublimating into something small, yet significant. The smokiness of Bengaluru, the vivaciousness of Koramangala—it felt so right.

For a moment, I let my mind wander forward. Coffee breaks, nights spent in long discussions, meeting each other at odd hours—it all seemed like a to-be reality now. I felt at ease, as I realized that we were not just classmates, but now each other's neighbours in this chaotic yet beautiful city.

'It looks like we will be seeing more of each other,' I said, hiding behind a smile not quite justifying the excitement I felt.

The next few days were filled with introductions, glimpses of the campus and a struggle to find our footing in the new chapter of our life. Come one, come all, I would say. I expected some despondent college vibe, but there was something different here. The students seemed determined and enthusiastic. The environment was infectious, and I was swept by it even though I missed my old comfortable ways.

The days went flying by, and before we knew it, we were already absorbed into our new college lives, with fresh names to talk to, fresh friends to make and humorous situations to balance out coddling with the 'norms' in academics! In between all this, Avantika and I slipped back into our comfortable space. Our conversations were filled with laughter and playful banter, with occasional serious talks about classes and future plans. We seemed to have begun from where we left off, now tinted by the shades of our shared experiences in Bengaluru.

But this time, things were different. I, for one, was very clear about one thing—we were no longer just friends. The way she laughed, the way her gaze lingered on me while she spoke and even the way she tucked her hair behind her ear, everything was so different. More than ever, I felt drawn to her, as if each little trait of hers was amplified. Perhaps, it was because in the dark days of online classes, I'd watched and cherished her from afar; and now, in reality, she was more beautiful, more enchanting.

The ability not to accept the blossoming feelings building up in me for her had totally disappeared after that. I wanted something more than late-night phone conversations and amusing inside jokes. I wanted to pour my heart out in front of her, something deep and meaningful that she could hear straight from my heart, uncut and unfiltered, to see whether anything in her felt the same. One thought that came and lodged itself in my brain, and once set there, wouldn't leave, was— how to propose to her. But it had to be something different, something that nobody had asked yet. It had to be planned to perfection.

In my PG room, I paced up and down, conjuring up all sorts of alternative scenarios in my disordered mind. Should it be simple? Something grand? Avantika deserved something extraordinary. I could feel the excitement bubbling up, but I was also nervous. I didn't want to rush this.

That's when I decided to call Tanishka. Maybe she could help me figure out the perfect way to propose. I dialled her number, and as soon as she picked up, I blurted out, 'Hey, Tanishka. I need your help. I'm going to propose to Avantika. I'm sure of it—I'm in love with her.'

There was a pause on the other end. Tanishka's voice came through, calm and collected, as always. 'Are you sure? Take your time before you do anything. Make sure it's really what you want.'

I felt a flicker of frustration. Why did she always seem so protective of Avantika when it came to me? It was like she didn't trust me or didn't believe in what I felt. I wondered for a second, *Why doesn't Tanishka want me to be with Avantika?*

I sat on the edge of my bed, gripping my phone a little tighter. Tanishka's voice was soft but firm, and it made me pause.

'What do you mean, take my time? I've been thinking about this for months now, Tanishka. I've liked her since the first day we started talking, and now . . . now it feels like the right time,' I said, pacing again.

'I know, but sometimes what feels right isn't always . . . well, right,' she replied.

'Okay, fine. Thanks for your time,' I said abruptly, feeling more frustrated than before. I hung up and tossed my phone aside.

After a few minutes of sitting in silence, I did what any modern-day romantic would do—I opened YouTube and typed in: *How to propose to a girl.*

The first video that popped up had this guy pulling off some grand gesture with roses and candles.

Arey, yeh sab toh bahut mehenga hai, I thought, shaking my head.

I stopped the video and leaned back on my bed, staring at the ceiling. *Yaar,* naturally *kuch sochna padega.*

I typed the message, 'Can we meet tomorrow at Ace Café after class?' and hit 'send' before I could second-guess myself. *'Whatever happens, I'll just say it the best I can,'* I thought, feeling a mix of nerves and excitement.

I opened my wardrobe and scanned it for a good shirt. Something nice, but not too obvious. I grabbed one, spritzed some of my best cologne and, with all these thoughts swirling in my mind, I finally managed to fall asleep.

The next morning, I woke up at around 7:30 a.m. and got myself ready just in time for the 8:30 a.m. class. The lectures felt boring, yet again, maybe because my mind was somewhere else entirely; I kept thinking about what I was about to do.

Avantika casually asked, 'Hey, what's going on? Why are we meeting at the Café? Should we also call Tanishka?'

I rapidly shook my head. 'No, just you and me,' I replied, my heart now beginning to jump a little.

So we met at Ace Café and ordered coffee. I could feel my heartbeat rising with each passing moment. I acted casual on the outside, but inside, I was far from it.

There I was, sitting beside her, staring into her eyes. Everything around us seemed to fade away, and all I could see was Avantika, more beautiful in this moment than I had ever realized.

I took a deep breath and said, 'Avantika . . . A pretty name that suits its bearer.' My voice trembled with a slightly tiny flutter. But that was about it.

'I've held this for so long, waiting for the right moment to tell you. But somewhere sitting here with you, I have realized . . . that there never is a perfect moment because, with you, every moment just feels perfect.'

I could feel my pulse quickening as I took a step even closer, the air heavy with the weight of everything I needed to say. 'At first, I was attracted to your beauty. But as I got to know you, it became evident that you weren't exactly that kind of girl. Not because of what you look like but rather from all that which is you: Your smile lost in thought, the twinkle in your eyes when you talk passionately about something, the way you make me feel like there is nothing else in the world that matters.'

I felt the strangest mix of emotions well up inside me as I took a pause, swallowed the lump forming in my throat and blurted it out: 'Avantika . . . I love you.

Not in the way they show in movies, but in a way that makes me want to be a better person for you. I love the way you challenge me, the way you care and how you make everything a little brighter. And I don't want to go through another day without you knowing that.'

I took her hand gently, holding it as if it were the most precious thing in the world. 'I don't know what the future holds, but I know that with you, everything feels possible. So here I am, sitting in front of you, hoping you'll feel the same way. Hoping that maybe, just maybe, I can be the one to make you as happy as you've made me.'

Her eyes softened, the world stood still and, in that moment, I knew that no matter what she said, everything was about to change forever.

Before I could delve deeper, I noticed my drink was over. I stared at the glass in front of me, the dim light casting a faint glow around the room. I poured myself another drink, the liquid splashing into the glass, a brief moment of comfort before the thoughts came flooding back.

'If only I'd listened to Tanishka back then,' I muttered, half to myself. 'She was trying to protect me in her own way, giving me all the signs . . . but no. I was too blinded by what I thought was love. Too much of a dumbass to see it.'

The weight of it hit me then. This wasn't just a memory; it was a reminder of the mistakes I made— the ones that shaped everything after. The Old Monk burned my throat, but it was nothing compared to the regret simmering inside.

A Rain-Kissed Confession

As the alcohol coursed through my veins, memories of the evening in 2020 surfaced. When Avantika said 'yes' to my proposal, I felt different kinds of feelings, a mix of relief and joy. Her words were soft yet firm and had left me in a daze. 'I don't know if it's love,' she said, 'but you're someone who helps me enjoy life and someone I cherish deeply.'

I couldn't believe it. I had a girl; it was like a dream wrapped in the warmth of our moments together. But Avantika made it clear: 'Let's keep this personal,' she said. 'These are our early days. I want to savour them without the world's eyes.'

We stepped out of the café into the night. There was a hint of rain in the sky with a cool breeze; the weather was as cosy as it could get. With just the two of us on the quiet street, it felt like a scene straight out of a movie. The heavens seemed to be holding their breath as we walked hand in hand.

Our PG was a twelve-minute walk. Soon, raindrops began to fall. At first, it was just a light drizzle, but soon it turned into a steady, gentle shower. The rain made everything feel fresh and new, like a promise of something magical.

We strolled slowly, our hands clasped together, feeling the rain soak through our clothes. The street was almost empty, with only the distant glow of streetlights and the occasional flicker of neon signs. We turned into a particularly isolated lane as the raindrops grew stronger.

We found shelter under the awning of a closed shop, where the only sounds were the rhythmic pattern of the rain that created a curtain of sound that added to the sense of intimacy.

We stood there, our bodies close, the warmth of our breaths mingling in the cool night air. I looked into Avantika's eyes, seeing them shine with a mix of excitement and affection. We were close enough that I could feel her breath on my face, warm and soft against the cool rain.

I tilted my head slightly, closing the distance between us. My fingers gently brushed her wet hair away from her face, my thumb caressing her cheek. She moved closer, her lips just a breath away from mine.

With our faces inches apart, I felt her warm breath mingling with mine. I leaned in, our lips meeting in a slow, deliberate kiss. The rain continued to fall around us, each drop adding to the sense of intimacy and connection.

Our kiss began softly, exploring the newness of this moment. Her lips were tender and responsive, matching the rhythm of my own. As we continued, the kiss deepened, becoming more passionate.

Soon we left for her PG.

We hadn't uttered a word since the kiss and, honestly, it wasn't necessary. The silence between us was comfortable, filled with the kind of understanding that needed no explanation. I watched her disappear inside before turning to make my way back to my own PG.

Once I was back, I took off my soaked clothes, the night's rain still fresh in my mind. I grabbed my phone, wiping off the droplets that collected on it. I stood still for a moment, lost in thought, with everything playing inside my head. The kiss . . . it was beyond what I imagined.

My phone buzzed softly, but before checking the notifications, I messaged Avantika, 'It was the best kiss ever.'

Her reply almost came instantly: 'Not really . . .'

I looked at the message for a second, not knowing whether to laugh or feel shy. And before I had time to brood over it, another message came in saying, 'But not bad either.' I couldn't help but smile at my screen.

When Everything Felt Like a Fairy Tale

Days passed, and we found ourselves talking more and more. The classes kept rolling. I was enjoying everything like never before. It felt like I had hit the jackpot—a great college, new friendships and Avantika. It was like living in a dream.

But they say, *'Even the sweetest dreams have their nightmares.'*

We kept things low-key in college, acting like we were just friends. Even Tanishka, who usually had a sixth sense for these things, was clueless. She'd asked me more than once if I had finally proposed to Avantika, and each time, I'd brush it off with a casual, 'No, not yet.' We never really talked much about it, so she never pushed me for more details.

Then, just as everything seemed to be picking up pace and everyone was getting involved in the hustle-bustle of daily life, the second wave of COVID hit. We hadn't even lived two complete months of the 'normal' when it all came crashing down again. Restrictions tightened, and the campus closed. Everything was to move back to the online mode again. The world suddenly felt *small* again—reduced to video calls and endless notifications.

Before we headed back to our hometowns, we decided to spend one last day together—just the three of us. It wasn't some grand plan, just a way to hold on to the time we had left. I invited Avantika and Tanishka to my PG since I had a single room, and it felt more personal than any café or park. We wanted to make the most of the time before heading back to the uncertainty that awaited us with the second wave looming.

That day, something unexpected happened. As we were sitting around, talking about everything and nothing, Avantika casually pulled out a cigarette. I blinked, completely taken aback. She lit it with ease, taking a drag, and all I could do was stare.

Tanishka didn't react, which made me wonder—*had she known about this the whole time?* I, on the other hand, had no idea.

'Wait . . . you smoke?' I finally asked, trying to keep my voice neutral.

Avantika smiled, blowing out a puff of smoke. 'Yeah, sometimes. Didn't think it was a big deal.'

It wasn't like I was judging her, but it was strange seeing her do something I had never associated with her. I'd never imagined her as the kind of person who smoked. And, to be honest, I hated the smell of cigarettes.

I shifted a little, feeling uneasy but trying to hide it. 'I don't know,' I said, feeling a little awkward. 'I've always disliked the smell.'

She looked at me, sensing my discomfort. 'You've never smoked, have you?' she said, with playful horror in her voice.

'Nope. Never thought I would. It's just not my thing,' I said, attempting to keep it light, but the smell was already getting to me.

She shrugged and took another drag. 'Don't worry, I'm not going to push you into anything.'

I smiled, but internally, I was still grappling with this new side of her. It felt like a piece of a puzzle that didn't match.

Ahh, fuck. Here I am, lighting the sixth cigarette of the day.

I stared at the small flame as it flickered on the tip of the cigarette, the irony not lost on me. Two years ago, I couldn't stand the smell, and now . . . now it's become a habit I can't shake.

Funny how habits stay, but people always find a way to leave.

Hidden Cards

The evening was light, easy and everything we needed. We played UNO, laughter filled the room as we threw down our cards and ordered cheese crust pizza— Avantika's favourite.

'You're cheating!' Tanishka yelled, as she threw a pillow at Avantika, who was smugly stacking up her cards.

'I never cheat. I'm just better,' she replied, her eyes glowing with a playful competitiveness.

Everything was spot on—one of those rare moments where one feels as if the world is pausing for you, letting you live in it a little longer. We laughed and teased each other, and for a while, it felt like nothing else mattered.

But then I noticed something out of the corner of my eye. Avantika's phone lit up. Mehul—the name flashed across the screen, and for a second, the air around me felt heavier. Mehul, her ex. I tried not to let it bother me, tried to focus on the game, but curiosity clawed inside me.

She quickly declined the call, and brushed it off like it didn't matter. But there was something in the way she looked at her phone—hesitant, distracted. She kept glancing at it, as if she was waiting for something. My mind started racing with questions. Why was he calling her? Why didn't she tell me about it? Were they still in touch? But I didn't ask. Not then. I wasn't sure if I wanted to know the answers.

'Hey, put down your phone,' I said, in a casual tone. 'Focus on the game. We have to gang up on Tanishka, or she's going to win again.'

Avantika smiled and placed her phone face down on the table. 'Yeah, yeah, I'm here,' she said, but her eyes flew back to her phone screen again. She was texting someone—perhaps him?—and that night, it felt like there was a wall between us, a wall I hadn't seen until then.

I reminded myself to remain present and to keep the tone light. But something was different, a slight fissure that I could not fully overlook. Still, I kept my mouth shut, praying it was nothing. Just a call. Just a text.

But somewhere in my heart, I knew something wasn't right.

Later in the night, Avantika suggested we go out to get beer. Now, I'd never had a beer in my life, but naturally, I nodded like a pro. We walked down to the shop near my PG, and as I stood in front of the fridge, it felt as if I was standing in front of the last question of *Kaun Banega Crorepati*. I didn't know a single brand, so I just grabbed Budweiser because, well, it sounded familiar—like something I'd seen in a movie once.

We got back to my PG and, of course, Tanishka took charge like she'd been doing this her whole life.

She popped open all our bottles with one smooth motion while I stood there, pretending like I knew what was going on. I gave her a nod like, 'Yeah, that's how it's done,' but inside, I was just thankful she didn't ask me to do it.

'Cheers,' Tanishka said, her eyes sparkling as we sat down to watch a movie. The lights lowered, and the sound of the film played in the background, but we weren't really focused on what was happening on the screen

By then, we were a little buzzed, just enough to feel like we could loosen up a little. At some point, Tanishka got a call from her parents. She groaned, knowing she'd have to leave. 'I better go, or they'll freak out,' she said, standing up reluctantly. 'My PG's just a three-minute walk, so it's fine.'

Avantika and I waved her off, and just like that, we were alone. The hum of alcohol ran through my bones, and the space between us throbbed in a heavy silence. The film kept playing, but neither of us was really watching it anymore. I turned to Avantika, her face lit by the dim glow of the screen, and before I knew it, I had reached for her, and enveloped her in an embrace. Her body fit against mine perfectly, as if this moment had been waiting for us all along.

Her eyes met mine, and something unspoken passed between us—a silent agreement that words weren't needed. Our lips met again, but this time, it was different. The kiss was slow at first, delicate, like we were exploring something fragile. Then, the intensity grew, as if all the feelings we had kept bottled up were suddenly free. The beer, the laughter, the warmth of the night—it all blended into something primal and real.

I pulled her closer, my hands finding her waist, and she complied, fingers threading through my hair, gently tugging me in, as if she couldn't get enough. Every touch sent electric jolts through our skin.

We collapsed on to the bed, still wrapped around each other. My fingers wandered to her back, around the curves of her body, I pulled her towards me. Her breath felt warm on my neck as she let out a soft gasp and gripped my shirt. There was no time for hesitation, and no space between us, just overwhelming need. The way she kissed me—slow, then fast and desperate—made my heart race. My hands slid under her top, feeling the warmth of her skin beneath my fingers, and I could feel her body tremble against mine. Her hands weren't idle either, tracing the lines of my shoulders, my chest, like she was memorizing every inch of me.

Her lips trailed down my neck, biting and leaving a trail of fiery sensation that sent shivers through me. I pulled her tighter, not wanting the moment to end. Every touch felt amplified, every kiss more intense than the last, as if the world outside didn't matter anymore. Our moans filled the room with the quiet hum of desire, and nothing else existed in the space.

We finally slowed down after what seemed like hours. As her head lay on my chest, I allowed her warm skin to linger upon mine. The silence was comfortable, but my mind had a million thoughts racing through it again, slowly coming back to me as the heat of the moment wore off.

Lying there, reality started to creep back in and with it came my thoughts that went to places I didn't want them to go.

I swallowed, unsure if this should come out of my mouth, but somehow the words had slipped out, soft and unenthusiastic. 'Do you keep in touch with Mehul?' I whispered—not quietly enough though, to break the stillness between us.

She glanced at me, hesitating for a moment to say, 'Yeah, we're just normal friends. We talk sometimes because he's a family friend.'

I frowned and tried to understand it. 'Is it even possible for an ex to be a friend?' I thought aloud, expecting a response that would give me peace, but she shrugged, unbothered by my curiosity.

Then she asked, 'Can I light a cigarette? You know, a cigarette after sex is something different.'

I raised an eyebrow, half in jest, 'Really? Is it really that special?'

She smirked. 'Give me the pack and the lighter off the table first, and then maybe you'll find out.'

I handed her the pack of cigarettes and lighter reluctantly. She quickly lit one and took a long, slow puff. She extended it to me, and against every instinct telling me to say no, I thought—why not? One try wouldn't hurt.

I took the cigarette, trying to act casual, but as soon as I inhaled, it felt as if my throat was on fire. I coughed uncontrollably, as my eyes watered. 'Oh god! How do people enjoy this? It's like licking car exhaust!'

Avantika chuckled, clearly amused by my struggle. 'Not everyone's made for it,' she teased.

'Yeah, no thanks,' I said, shaking my head, still recovering from the aftertaste.

It's 2024, and I'm sitting here, watching the smoke lazily swirl from my lips, the warm buzz of my sixth peg settling in. Who would've thought I'd be this person? Smoking has become essential for me.

I glance at my phone lying next to me, its screen lighting up with notifications. *100+ unread messages*. Group assignments, deadlines, reminders—it's the MBA life on steroids. I stare at them for a second and swipe them away. Honestly, *kabhi kabhi toh mujhe bhi* free-riding *karna chaiye*. Let someone else take the wheel for once. Isn't that what an MBA is all about? Delegation, right?

But then, another notification catches my eye—*Tanishka*. It's a message I've been avoiding to reply. I open it, and there it is:

'Live your life; don't get stuck on me.
'I'm removing you from Instagram and Snapchat. If you ever need anything, just let me know. I'll always be here for you.
'Goodbye and good luck for your placement.'

I watch the words as they hang there. They took a long time to sink in. Interesting how times change and people drift apart. I have another sip and the impact of these words hit my chest.

I know I need to respond, and at last, I do: 'You are the one who told me not to get stuck on people. And yeah, this time, I'm ready for that. All the best for your next two years at St. Xavier's. Take care, Tanishka.'

Suddenly, it hit me—I should've just listened to Tanishka's words. If only I had understood what she was trying to say before everything slipped away. Before I made that move, before I . . . proposed.

But I didn't.

If I hadn't proposed to Avantika, maybe things would have been different. I ended up losing Tanishka not once, but twice, once because of Avantika, and the second . . . for reasons I still don't fully understand. It's like there was something hidden, something I wasn't meant to know, and now it haunts me.

I slid my phone and glanced at the time—12:00 a.m. Ah, 12 already. Who even sleeps at 12 during an MBA? It's practically midday in MBA time. The night was young, and my mind? Restless as ever.

I couldn't stop thinking about it all, so I let my thoughts wander back.

Unanswered Calls and Unspoken Words

With the night of high emotions and intimacy behind us, I dropped Avantika off at her PG and returned to mine. The evening's passion and the unfiltered-ness of our energy somehow clung on to me as I dropped on my bed, completely exhausted and thinking: 'What's the next day's story gonna be?'

We had our flights scheduled for the afternoon, so we headed to the airport together. As I boarded the flight, my mind couldn't help but wander back to the past couple of months. So much had happened, I thought about how the next two years might play out, with excitement bubbling inside me.

But as soon as I landed, the familiar WebEx notifications started flooding in. Our college life was back on our laptops—back to virtual reality. Things between Avantika and I seemed perfect, though. We had small fights here and there, but nothing major. Everything felt stable. Except, I didn't have anyone to talk to about it, about us. She made it clear that we were to keep it quiet.

I couldn't even tell Tanishka. She had warned me not to propose to her, and yet, I had. Plus, Avantika and Tanishka were really close. If Tanishka found out, she might tell Avantika, and then . . . Well, that would be a mess.

Avantika and I used to talk every night. We shared everything, but one night, it was different. Her phone was busy when I tried her, and I assumed she'd call me back in a few minutes. Two hours passed, and still no word from her. I called again, but no reply. Worried, I messaged Tanishka, asking if she was talking to Avantika, but she wasn't.

It took me three hours to finally learn why. Avantika had been with Mehul, helping him cope with the weight of his academic stress. I'd never seen that side of her before. And there I was, stuck in my own head, waiting in the dark.

As I sat with that silence, it ate away at me—a low itch I couldn't shake. I felt there was a subtext to this, a silence, words between the words, more to the story than I understood yet, more waiting to be uncovered.

Although I was trying to process the idea of an ex remaining friends, it was tough to digest. The thought sat heavy, tangled with questions I couldn't untangle— was I overthinking, or was there something hidden beneath the surface?

Secrets and Silence

The following morning, during a particularly monotonous WebEx lecture, my phone vibrated. It was Avantika.

'Hey, I'm really sorry about yesterday. You didn't respond to my messages. Is everything alright?'

I quickly typed back, 'I already told you everything is okay. I hope Mehul is feeling better now?'

'Yeah, he's doing better now. He doesn't really have too many friends besides me, so it was important that I spoke with him.' I understood why she had been distracted and nodded, 'It's fine.'

After a short silence, I said, 'We've been dating for over a month. Could we share this with other folks like Tanishka or Pavni or Saurabh?'

I could hear the hesitation as she replied, 'I'm not comfortable with that. Let's just keep it between you and me for now.'

We talked with ease and casualness, and all felt fairly normal between us—at least, that's how it felt on the surface.

Over the following months, I learned more things about Avantika's past and the motivation for some of her choices. She shared her most personal secrets—stories about family issues, personal struggles and everything in between.

As the second wave subsided, the Karnataka government declared that colleges would open in hybrid mode. It brought relief, mixed with some uncertainty for what the future entailed as we navigated our way into this new dimension of our lives.

The Pressing Question?

We scheduled a Zoom meeting to find an answer to the most pressing question at the moment: Do we stay at home and wait for a third wave to make its grand entrance, or should we be bold and travel back to Bengaluru and face whatever came our way?

Avantika began, 'I'll come to Bengaluru, if and only if it's absolutely necessary. Otherwise, I don't mind being cosy and staying at home.'

Tanishka, ever the thrill-seeker, countered with a grin, 'I'm going for sure! I'm over this home quarantine life. I am craving some actual human interaction and a change in scenery.'

I found myself in a dilemma, the inertia and the comfort of staying home was strong and urging me to stay at home, but the magnetic pull of the campus life that awaited me was stronger and calling me out. I felt restless and eager to escape the limitations of my existing routine and immerse myself in the vibrant energy of college life again. Should I share this longing with Avantika, or was it better to keep it to myself? I pondered over the dilemma, feeling the tug-of-war between my head and my heart. There was a voice inside me urging me to follow my heart, reminding me, 'Listen to your heart, it knows what's best for you.'

Despite the doubts, I listened to that inner voice. I wanted to make the most of this chance—the chance to laugh with friends, form lifelong bonds and enjoy the freedom that awaited me. This was my chance to live it all. I had made my decision: I was going.

I was all set and ready to go but Avantika wasn't exactly happy about it. Right after the meeting, she sent me a text, *'Haan, jaa. Mujhe chhod ke* college enjoy *kar. Main yaha* online classes *mein hi marti hu. Tu waha maze maar.'*

I sniggered at her sarcastic comment, but I could feel that she was genuinely upset. Irrespective, I had made up my mind. I wanted to experience college, even if it meant upsetting her a little.

Guess Who Is Back Again

Bengaluru, again. Along with the masks and social distancing, again. This time, there was something about the city that felt refreshing. Offline classes had resumed and, despite the oddity of attending lectures in person with half our faces covered, it felt . . . good.

Slowly and steadily, we all settled into the routine of campus life, but there was still a part of me that couldn't shake the thought of Avantika. I missed her. Even though I enjoyed the company of Pavni and my batchmates, somewhere deep down, something was nagging me—Avantika's absence.

Then, just two days later, Tanishka arrived in Bengaluru. We didn't talk much—there was always this unspoken distance between us. Most of our conversations revolved around studies, nothing personal. Without Avantika in the mix, we had run out of things to say. We'd sit together in class, exchange a few words about assignments, but that was it. No depth, no real connection.

Meanwhile, things with Avantika had taken a strange turn. Ever since I had returned back to Bengaluru, her messages had become shorter, and she wasn't talking to me as much. I assumed she was upset that I had decided to come back. Whenever we spoke, she would throw in remarks like, 'Making more friends there, huh? Why would you even remember me?' I'd reassure her, but deep down, I could feel something was off.

The same thing happened again at night—her call was busy. I didn't ask for any explanation and let it slide. This time too, I found out it was Mehul. He was going through a lot of academic pressure, and once again, she was there for him. I wouldn't say that I was jealous . . . but it wasn't easy to digest either.

Days went by, and it became a pattern. Twice a week, she'd talk to Mehul for hours, leaving me with just a message saying, 'Mehul is going through something.'

The Confession

It had been a few weeks and the late-night calls between Avantika and Mehul continued. It slowly started to wound me. It wasn't that I was ultra-orthodox or insecure, but having regular conversations with an ex? That was just something I couldn't stomach anymore. It felt like an imaginary line had been crossed and I needed to talk to someone about it. The only person who truly knew both Avantika and me was Tanishka and, at this point, no one else felt like a better choice.

It was eating away at me, and it just couldn't stay in me any longer. At last, one day, I confessed everything to Tanishka. Her first words were, 'I told you to take more time, but you were too blinded by love to listen.'

I sighed, aware she was right. 'What do I do now?' I asked, hoping for some sort of clarification.

'Nothing,' she replied. 'Just talk it out.'

After that, I started sharing everything with Tanishka. She became my confidant, like no one else in my life, this one-person filter, telling her all about the ups and downs with Avantika. As the hybrid classes continued and the government announced that mandatory classes would resume in December, I had three months left before the real grind began again. During this phase, Tanishka and I grew closer, learning more about each other. But no matter how close we became, she never revealed any secrets about Avantika—just best friends' boundaries.

Tanishka became my safe space, the person I could turn to when everything felt too overwhelming.

The Midnight Anticipation

It was October again—my birthday month—and yet, the one person I wanted to celebrate with wasn't there—Avantika. I missed her more than I could admit, but all I had was Tanishka to celebrate with. On my birthday night, I sat in my room, staring at my phone, waiting for Avantika to call. Maybe she'd surprise me with a cake, or maybe she'd come. But when the hours passed, nothing happened. No calls, no texts. As I waited, I was lost in that awkward limbo of whether to continue to wait or to call her up. Then, at 11:34, there was a knock on my door. My heart skipped a beat—I thought that maybe it was something Avantika had sent. But when I opened it, it was Tanishka, standing there with a cake box in one hand and a black plastic bag in the other.

'Are you going to leave me standing out here, or can I come in?' she teased, grinning.

I masked my disappointment, for I was expecting someone else. 'Oh sure, come in,' I said, beaming as she brought in the cake. I thanked her for being there.

By the time it hit midnight, my phone started ringing with calls and texts from everyone—except the one person I was waiting for. Her absence stung, and I tried to hide it, but Tanishka could tell.

'You don't seem happy,' Tanishka said, reading me like a book. 'What's wrong?'

I sighed. 'I am waiting for Avantika's call . . . I am feeling very anxious. It has already crossed midnight.'

Tanishka shrugged and smiled. 'She's probably asleep, don't mind it.'

Then, she fished out two Budweiser cans from the black plastic bag and said, 'Come on, let's celebrate! It's your birthday. Forget everything for now.'

We sat and drank and talked for hours. At that moment, something shifted—I began to realize how much I depended on Tanishka. She was more than a friend; she was becoming my best friend. We laughed, we reminisced, but at the back of my head, I was still waiting for that call from Avantika.

Then, I noticed Tanishka's phone buzzing. She glanced at the screen—it was Avantika calling. I raised my eyebrows, asking her to put it on speaker.

She hesitated but eventually did. The moment the call connected, we heard Avantika's voice, sounding stressed, '*Yaar,* a major fuck-up happened. I was talking to Mehul and forgot to call Dev for his birthday.' My heart sank.

She quickly turned off the speaker and rushed outside. When she came back, she said, 'Avantika was just talking to Mehul about some family issue. Relax, nothing major.'

I didn't believe her. I looked at her and said quietly, 'Tell me the truth . . . please.'

'Are they dating again?' I asked, my voice barely hiding the frustration. She shook her head, trying to calm me down. 'Nah, chill out. Just finish your beer. We'll talk about this tomorrow. She's your girlfriend, right? You chose her.'

Before I could respond, my phone rang. It was Avantika. I hesitated but picked it up, putting it on speaker.

'Sorry, Dev . . . I don't know how I fell asleep like that,' she said, her voice sweet but hurried. 'Happy birthday, my love. I'm so sorry. I've sent you a gift, and it'll be there tomorrow.'

Tanishka gave me a look, silently urging me not to mention what I'd overheard earlier.

'It's okay,' I said, trying to mask the hurt. 'Good night.'

As soon as I hung up, my eyes could not help— tears started welling up, and Tanishka noticed. She didn't say anything at first, just quietly wiped them away. I couldn't hold it in any longer.

'I love her, Tanishka . . . I still love her. But why these lies? Why all this?'

Tanishka sighed, placing her hand on my shoulder. 'Okay, listen . . . if I tell you something, you won't tell Avantika, right?'

'I promise,' I said, my voice calm in contrast to the storm that raged in my body.

'She tells me they're just friends, but honestly, I have no idea why she talks to Mehul that much. And Mehul . . . he's not over her. There may be something else too. He even came to visit her recently.'

My heart sank further. 'How do you know that?'

Tanishka hesitated. 'I follow Mehul on Instagram. Here, look.' She pulled out her phone and showed me a post—Mehul and Avantika, together. Mehul, with his awkward smile and those oversized glasses, stood next to Avantika, who looked as beautiful as ever.

'Who posts pictures with their ex like this?' I muttered, feeling a mix of anger and disbelief.

'Forget it. Trust Avantika,' Tanishka said, trying to reassure me. 'Finish your beer.'

After a pause, Tanishka broke the tension with an unexpected question. 'You do realize that we weren't this close, right? But these last few months have been . . . should we be best friends?'

I stared at her, startled by the directness of her question. 'Yeah, Tanishka. I want us to be best friends. Thank you for everything.'

We talked throughout the night, about everything: our first crushes, our most embarrassing moments, the first people we'd kissed. There were no walls, there were no filters. We laughed, drank more beer and told stories we hadn't shared with anyone else.

And then, something happened—something unspoken. It wasn't loud or obvious, but it was enough to shift the dynamic, adding something more to our trio. Tanishka made me promise not to mention it to anyone.

And, well, promises are meant to be kept.

It is 2024, and I am sitting with a half-drained glass. As I am about to pour myself another one, I realize that the Old Monk is gone—just like that.

I look at the empty bottle, sigh and look at the time—
2 a.m. How did it get so late again? The ghosts of 2021
came flooding back like shadows that never end. It
amuses me how time can fog everything except for the
moments you'd like to forget.

The girl who had been my anchor through the
storms, the one who shared countless late nights and
whispered secrets with me, was now just a fragment
of my past.

All night, the weight of it pressed down on me
as I sipped the remnants of my drink. The promises,
the unuttered words, how we thought we knew each
other—these were the things that remained. Those
memories were timeless—a beautiful, sad landscape
carved in the places in my head.

This time, I tried setting seven alarms in the hope
that I might finally wake up on time. The first alarm
went off at 10 a.m.—snooze. 10:05—snooze again.
By 10:10, I was alert enough to think, 'Oh crap,
I have a 10:30 class.' Classic MBA move—living life
dangerously between snooze buttons and deadlines.

Feeling oddly refreshed (thanks, Old Monk—my
body's probably adjusted to it), I made my way to Prof
Ronit's stats class. There he was, teaching T-tests . . .
on pen and paper. In an MBA. I mean, who are we?
Statisticians from the Stone Age?

On Excel, it's three clicks. But here we were,
burning through two full pages of calculations like
cavemen discovering fire. I always wanted to raise my
hand and ask, 'Sir, which company in 2024 is going
to say, "Forget automation—grab that notepad and

manually solve this T-test"?' Because that's a job I'd love to miss out on.

His voice droned on like a radio stuck between stations—just the kind of frequency that makes you question every life decision. I glanced around, and sure enough, about 50 per cent of the class was either half-asleep or on the verge of it.

But honestly, I was pretty relaxed after seeing all the others. MBA now means *relative marking*. And in MBA language, that translates to 'you're not just competing against yourself—you're competing against every other person in that room. So even if you scored a solid ninety, but everyone else scored 100, well, congratulations, you just failed'.

I thought an MBA was supposed to be about teamwork and growth, you know? Learning together, building synergy, all that corporate jazz. But nope! Here we were, a bunch of over-caffeinated gladiators in a statistical death match, racing to see who could finish the T-test first. Because, obviously, McKinsey is looking for people who can win the fastest pen-and-paper T-test champions.

'Congratulations, you nailed that manual calculation! Now grab your notepad and welcome to the prestigious "Manual Math Division"' . . . Finally, after what felt like an eternity, the class ended. Sweet relief—until I remembered there were still two more subjects ahead, none of which made sense to me, ever.

After surviving all those lectures, I couldn't shake the thought: Was this B-school stuck in 2024 or had it time-travelled from the 1990s? Someone really needed to remind them that laptops and computers were not just a dream but actual tools used in this century.

I finally made my way back to my room. The silence of the hallway felt like a relief, a break from the constant noise of the day. As I reached for my keys and slid them into the lock, my fingers brushed against the key ring. That little key ring. The one Tanishka had gifted me.

I paused for a moment, staring at it—the charm dangling there, catching the faint light. It was small, barely noticeable to anyone else, but to me, it carried the weight of a thousand memories.

I knew I liked her—more than I was ever willing to admit—but did that mean our friendship had to suffer? Can two people not stay best friends just because one of them felt something more?

As I held that key ring in my hand, I couldn't help but think about how things had unfolded between us. It was Tanishka who first felt something for me, but back then, I was with Avantika. I was too wrapped up in that mess to even realize what was happening with Tanishka. She kept her feelings hidden, buried under the weight of our so-called friendship.

And when things finally started to change—when I realized I felt the same—she had already moved on with someone else. Timing has always been our worst enemy.

It made me wonder—did loving someone always mean risking the friendship? Or, was it just bad luck that every time one of us was ready, the other was too late?

It was like a cruel joke—falling for each other, but never at the right time.

The Unspoken Moments

I won't forget my birthday in the year 2020. That was the year I found Avantika. But 2021? That's when I found something even more precious—my best friend, Tanishka.

Days blurred into weeks, and every day, Tanishka and I grew closer. The late-night talks, the constant banter—it felt so natural, so destined. The more we talked, the less I longed for Avantika. There was something strange about how that void started to fill itself up without me even really noticing.

We'd always fight over the strangest things. I'd look at her and say: 'How do you even watch anime? It's just cartoons!' And she would shoot back without missing a beat, 'And how do you watch Shah Rukh Khan in every film? Same overacting, same running with his arms wide open for drama!'

I had to admit, she had a point. The whole arms-wide-open SRK signature move was kind of ridiculous when you thought about it. But it didn't stop me from defending him.

One thing I always admired about Tanishka was how unfiltered she was. She never sugar-coated anything, and that honesty was rare. She never lied—well, except for that one time. That one lie that changed everything.

The Distance between Us

Avantika was in my life then and, though things felt shaky, I was holding on, hoping that maybe—just maybe—she wasn't lying. That Mehul was just her friend, nothing more. But by the time December rolled in, it wasn't just Avantika occupying my mind anymore. It was also Tanishka.

Yet, every time I brought up Avantika, Tanishka would either ignore it or change the subject. I couldn't tell if it was deliberate or just my imagination.

There was this particular day I remember when we were sitting in the library. The silence felt louder than usual, and I could sense something weighing on her mind. After a while, she just looked at me, eyes searching for something deeper.

'Basu,' (she used to call me by this nickname. I still have no clue why. I mean, out of all the nicknames in the world, *Basu*?) she said quietly, 'what's your priority list?'

I blinked, surprised by the question. 'Huh?'

'And in your life, who comes first? Avantika or me?'

I froze. The space between us thickened with the gravity of her question. I knew the answer, but to say it out loud would be betraying Tanishka even if it was the truth. 'Tanishka . . . she's my girlfriend,' I said slowly, as if apologizing. 'So, yeah, she comes first.'

The words hung in the air for a moment before she nodded. There was no argument, no outburst. Just a quiet nod, as if she had already known what I was going to say.

'Oh then,' she whispered, 'we can't be best friends anymore. Not like this.'

I felt panic swell in my chest. 'What? No, Tanishka, that's not what I was saying. You're my best friend.'

'Basu, we can't do this anymore.' It was her voice that pierced the silence that had engulfed the library. Tanishka was sitting across, staring down at the table, as if tracing patterns on the wood, trying to block out what she was about to say.

I blinked, unsure of where this conversation was going. 'What do you mean?'

She looked up, and there was something in her gaze I hadn't seen before—an unfamiliar distance. 'I mean, with you and Avantika. I feel like . . . I'm always stuck in the middle, and January is coming and Avantika will be here.'

I opened my mouth to argue but fell short of words. The truth was, Tanishka had always been there for me, even when Avantika wasn't. Yet, I kept her in the background, not realizing how much I was hurting her.

She sighed and ran her fingers through her hair, frustration all over her face. 'I can't be your second choice, Basu.'

'No, you're not,' I replied quickly, but I didn't sound convincing. She shook her head. 'You don't get it. I asked you—what's your priority list? And you didn't even hesitate when you said it was Avantika.'

'And that's the problem,' she said, standing up abruptly. 'I can't keep doing this. I can't pretend like that. We're not on the same page.'

'Tanishka, wait,' I stood up, too, reaching out as if I could physically stop her from leaving. 'I don't want to lose you.'

She paused, clutching the back of her chair. 'You already have, Dev.'

I stood there paralysed by the words that came out of her mouth, as if some arrows made of words sliced through me. It was like she had dropped a bomb on me and before I could even think of a reply, she turned and stormed out of the library, leaving me there alone, surrounded by rows of silent books. It was as if the air had become heavier and the space suddenly too small, too suffocating.

The Quiet Drift

After that conversation in the library, all my time in Bengaluru became hazy. I couldn't escape the feeling that something was slipping through my fingers—no, someone, actually. Someone who had meant more to me than I was willing to admit, even to myself. The distance between us widened each time I attempted to mend things.

The hardest times were at night. My mind would race when I was by myself in the quiet. I would think back on Tanishka and our previous exchanges, wondering what went wrong . . . All of it seemed like a hazy memory now—the chats, the giggles, the comfort. I would spend hours lying awake, going over every phrase and every moment again in the hope of fixing it. But the answers never arrived, no matter how many times I reviewed it.

And then, after spending hours thinking about Tanishka, I'd do something that only made things worse—I'd text Avantika.

It was a habit I couldn't seem to break. 'I'm still talking to Avantika,' I'd tell myself, as if that would somehow make me feel better. Like it would fill the void, but I knew deep down that this wasn't the answer, that it was simply another diversion, another brittle bond I was attempting to maintain despite the fact that both seemed to be broken. was losing both of them, and I was too stubborn to admit it. I thought I could balance it all—my friendship with Tanishka, whatever was left of it, and whatever it was that I had with Avantika. But the truth was that I was losing them both.

When We Were Us

I kept trying.

Every day, I found myself reaching out, asking her to talk, to just explain what had gone wrong. 'We'll sort it out,' I would say. 'We can fix this. Just tell me what happened.'

But every time, she'd give me the same answer. A smile that didn't reach her eyes and a half-hearted 'It's fine.' I could feel her slipping further away, but I wasn't ready to give up. Not yet. I told myself that if I tried hard enough, if I kept pushing, we'd find our way back.

So, I kept at it. Day after day, I'd ask her to meet, to talk. I tried everything—random messages, sending her songs that once made us laugh. But nothing worked. The more I tried, the more distant she became. It was like chasing a shadow.

Finally, after what felt like a hundred failed attempts, we had a real conversation. It wasn't the heartfelt talk I had imagined, but it was something else. We were sitting in the canteen one afternoon and I managed to catch her alone.

'Will you please let us talk?' I asked, this time nearly begging. 'Discuss the problem with me. We can work things out. We usually do.'

With a sigh, she set down her plate and gave me a weary look. She seemed as if she was about to dismiss me once more, as she had done so many times in the past. But, this time, something was different. She didn't look away.

'Fine,' she said, her voice quieter than usual. 'We'll talk. But it's not going to change anything.'

'There's a difference between best friends and just friends. Best friends stay, no matter what. But regular friends . . . They drift apart. And sometimes, no matter how hard you try, you can't bring them back.'

Her words stung, but at least it was a start. I leaned in, desperate for any sliver of hope that we could fix this. 'Why does it feel like we're drifting apart?' I asked, my voice barely above a whisper.

Lifting her eyes to the table, she trailed her fingers along the edges of her plate, 'Because we are,' she said at last. 'I don't know when it happened, but we're just . . . not the same anymore.'

I felt a lump form in my throat. 'But we can fix it. We always figure things out. That we've gone through a lot together.'

Her eyes found mine and they were filled with a sadness that almost broke me as she slowly shook her head.

'Not this time. We're not reading from the same page anymore. We have not been for a long time.'

I didn't know what to say. I had been waiting so long, trying to convince myself things were going to get better, that we were going to go back to the way we used to be, if I just pushed through. But hearing her say it out loud . . . it broke something inside me.

I nodded, though every part of me wanted to argue, to fight. 'So that's it then?' I asked, my voice shaking. 'We're just . . . friends now?'

'Just friends,' she said softly. 'Like you and Pavni.'

And just like that, the final thread between us snapped.

The Moment It All Broke

Tanishka and I still talked, but it was different now. She never made the first move. I was the only one seeking her out, texting her, calling her, wondering if we could meet or if we could sit together in class. It was always me. She hardly ever answered the phone and when she did, it would feel like she was being made to, like she was really speaking to someone else—someone more important. We still spoke, but it was rare, almost robotic. By January, the distance between us had grown, and yet, I tried to ignore it.

January was a strange month. Avantika was coming back soon. I should've been excited. I should've felt something. But deep down, I knew things weren't the same. Sure, we were still dating, but there was this unsettling feeling I couldn't shake. We said, 'I love you', but it was hollow, like we were forcing ourselves to believe in something that wasn't there anymore.

Then came 7 January—Tanishka's birthday. I wanted to make things right, but there was this invisible wall between us.

Just two days later, Avantika would be landing in Bengaluru, and I was caught in this mess between what was and what should have been.

The Unfair Court of Friendship

7 January. I was ready—*really ready*—to make her birthday unforgettable. I had planned everything, down to the smallest detail. I was going to surprise her at 11:30 with a cake, just like she had surprised me once.

I reached her PG, my heart racing a bit, as I knocked on her door. She opened it, and there she was, sitting in her usual spot. I sat down next to her, a smile already forming on my face, ready for the moment.

But something was off.

She looked at me like there was something she needed to say, 'Basu, I need to tell you something.'

I smiled, trying to act casual, even though I felt a knot tightening in my stomach. 'Yeah, sure, tell me, Tanishka.'

'I'm in a relationship,' she said.

Her words hit harder than I could've ever imagined.

I wasn't prepared for the jealousy that followed. It crawled inside me, unexpected and raw. She was just my friend. My best friend. Yet, I felt this unbearable sting, as if I was losing something I didn't even realize I had.

'Who?' I asked, my voice barely above a whisper.

'He's coming to meet me now. You'll meet him too.'

Meet him? My heart sank. I didn't want to meet him. I didn't want to see the person who had taken her away. But how could I say no? I never could when it came to her.

I tried to act normal, as if it didn't bother me, but inside I was a mess. 'Why?' The word slipped out, and it wasn't even a question, more like a desperate plea. But what right did I have to ask? I was with Avantika, wasn't I? I was in a relationship, too. Yet, here I was, feeling like I was losing something much more important than I had ever realized.

At that moment, it hit me. A female best friend can either have a boyfriend or a best friend—but not both.

This should seriously be a law! Like a legitimate court order.

I felt like the sidekick in my own story, suddenly sidelined because someone else had entered the picture.

Before I could say anything more, there was a knock on the door. She got up to open it, and in walked this guy. A 6'1" gym freak, with muscles bulging out of a crumpled t-shirt that looked like it hadn't seen an iron in months. And those jeans? They were barely hanging on. Honestly, his whole vibe screamed, *'I don't care about basic hygiene, but I can bench press a car.'* The worst dressing sense I had ever seen. If I didn't know better, I would've thought he was a bouncer at some shady bar.

'Hey there, dude! I am Mihir,' he said with his remarkable Jat accent cutting through the air, rattling my sense of pride.

I plastered a smile on my face, barely holding together the pretence of courtesy. Inside, I was crumbling, as every word he uttered served as a stark reminder of all I was losing. It felt as if someone had flipped a switch; I was now a total outsider in a place I had once belonged.

I stood with her as she cut the cake. The first bite—I could tell she was perplexed—but she gave it to me. *Haan*, that was a sign. Maybe it felt like a sign. Maybe, just maybe, I still did mean something to her.

Meanwhile, Mihir stood there, staring at us like he was missing the point. I couldn't help but think: *Why the hell is he even here?* His whole presence felt like an intrusion, a reminder that things had changed.

The small talk that followed only made things worse. At one point, *mann kar raha tha ki jaake uska muh noch lu.* My hands were shaking, my thoughts spiralling into a chaotic mess of jealousy and anger.

After what felt like hours of forced smiles and fake laughter, I couldn't hold it in anymore.

I turned to him, trying my best to sound polite, 'Mihir, can you please come back later? I need to talk to Tanishka.'

He gave me a look like I had just insulted his entire family. Then, glancing at Tanishka, he said in his thick accent, 'It's her birthday, bro. I think I should be with her.'

I forced a smile, but inside I was losing it. *'Bhai, tu abhi abhi aaya hai.* Just leave for a bit.'

I knew what I was doing wasn't exactly right. I mean, I'd lose it if Avantika's best friend tried to pull this with me, but I didn't care. I needed to talk to her, and I couldn't wait anymore.

Mihir looked back at Tanishka, probably expecting her to throw me out or something, but she sighed and said, 'Fifteen minutes, Mihir. Please.'

He hesitated for a moment, his brow furrowing like he was trying to figure out if he should punch me or not. But finally, he nodded and left the room, muttering something under his breath that I didn't catch.

As soon as Mihir left the room . . .

'*Kya majboori thi tujhe isko* boyfriend *banane ki?*' The words came out almost instantly with frustration and jealousy laced in every syllable.

Tanishka turned to me, her expression unreadable. 'I didn't want to get caught in your mess with Avantika,' she said, her voice calm but firm. 'You never treated me like I mattered when she was around, Basu. Even when you were with Avantika, you barely talked to me. You know that, right? And she is coming the day after tomorrow and *mujhe phir se wahi* experience *nhi krna tha.*'

Her words struck me like the most agonizing stab I'd ever felt. But the worst of it? She was right. All this time, I had neglected her unintentionally, while I was unconsciously preparing her to be replaced by someone else. And now, I was paying for it.

'I don't want to see you with him!' I shouted before I could hold myself back, pure envy and aggravation rising in me.

Did the girl wince, even for a moment? No, not once. Her expression was cool, but her words cut through the air and hit me. 'You had a choice, Basu: me or Avantika. You made your choice.'

And there it was—the cold, harsh truth I had been avoiding all this time. I had made my choice. And, in doing so, I had lost her.

She took a deep breath, her voice softening just a little. 'I'm sorry,' she said, and this time, it wasn't an apology for anything she had done. It was for what I had done.

Her voice trembled slightly, and I could see the pain behind her eyes. 'I've already suffered too much, Basu. Mihir and I started dating yesterday. I can't go through this again, not knowing that you might just sideline me when Avantika comes back. I can't bear the thought of being pushed away again.'

Every word felt like a dagger twisting deeper into my heart. The jealousy I had felt earlier morphed into a new kind of ache—one that came from the realization that I had taken her for granted. I had been so wrapped up in my own confusion and feelings for Avantika that I hadn't considered what I was losing in the process.

'I don't want to see you hurt,' she continued, her voice steady despite the turmoil in her eyes. 'I can't keep waiting around for you to make a choice that's already been made. It hurts too much to be a second choice.'

Her words cut deeper than I thought was possible. I sat there, speechless, watching her, my heart shattering into pieces I knew I'd never be able to put back together.

Tanishka looked away and, for a moment, the silence between us felt louder than anything.

Fifteen minutes later, Mihir walked back in. For him, it seemed those fifteen minutes were plenty. I've always had a problem with people whose names start with 'M'—Mehul, Mihir, Manvit. It's like there's a universal rule for them to annoy me.

Mihir walked in and stared at me as if I had stolen his protein powder. '*Ho gaya?*' he asked in his thick Jat accent, breaking the uncomfortable silence.

Tanishka nodded, '*Haan.*'

And just like that, the air in the room froze. There was no conversation, nothing. We sat there quietly, as if waiting for something to happen. Mihir sat there like he was waiting for me to leave, and I was silently wondering when he would finally go. Tanishka, on the other hand, seemed like she regretted having us both meet in the first place.

I thought: *Maybe it's better if I go*. But I didn't want to leave, and when I finally stood up, ready to walk out, Tanishka spoke up, 'Where are you going?'

That question—it was a relief. At least she still wanted me there, for whatever little that was worth.

But Mihir? He didn't say anything, but I could feel his jealousy burning holes into the back of my head. His eyes screamed: *Why does this guy get to stay?*

A thought crossed my mind: 'Male best friends are practically designed to make boyfriends jealous.' And that day, I believed it more than ever.

Before I could process it further, Mihir finally broke the silence. '*Milte hain kal,*' he muttered through gritted teeth, barely able to conceal his irritation. And with that, he stormed out, slamming the door behind him.

The second the door closed behind him, something shifted. The air that had been thick with tension became soft, fragile. Tanishka and I looked at each other, and for the first time in months, it felt like we could actually talk.

And we did. We talked about everything. Every hidden feeling, every misunderstanding, every hurt. We cried together—long, painful tears that seemed to wash away all the unsaid words between us. It was like we were trying to heal wounds that were too deep.

And she promised me not to share with anyone and—promises are meant to be kept.

Then came the hardest part. Tanishka looked at me, her eyes wet with tears, and said, 'Basu, this is our last meeting. *Hum ab se nahi mil rahe hain.*'

The words shattered me. I couldn't believe what I was hearing. And just as if fate had a cruel sense of humour, her phone buzzed with a series of notifications. Mihir's name flashed across the screen repeatedly. His messages were pouring in like a flood, one after the other.

And all those messages were for me: *'Kitna c****ya hai tera best friend . . .'*

I couldn't help myself. I looked at her and said, *'Tu usko chhod de.* He doesn't deserve you, Tanishka. He's a lousy, insecure guy.'

'I know,' she said quietly.

Tanishka stayed quiet, her eyes focused on the messages, but she didn't respond. We both ignored the buzzing phone, pretending that it wasn't there.

I tried to salvage the situation. 'I'll talk to Avantika this time. I swear, things will be different.'

She just gave me a sad smile. 'Two boats? You're going to put your feet in two boats, Basu?'

And there it was—the truth I didn't want to admit, staring me in the face. She was right. I was trying to have it all, and in doing so, I was losing everything.

'Leave,' she said very softly, but firmly. 'Forget everything. Let us be strangers. Avantika will be back the day after tomorrow. You'll have her, and that will be enough, right? I can't do this anymore.'

I hesitated, my eyes scanning her face for an ounce of hope but found none. Just before I exited, she called out 'Basu, remember: love in moderation, okay? Don't pour it all in, otherwise you'll start to overlook others—your friends. And eventually, you'll find yourself alone.'

That was it; I had finally lost her. Not the way you lose someone to death but in a way that opens a hollow void, one that never truly feels whole again, no matter how hard you shove everything into it.

I walked out feeling as heavy as a ton of bricks. I lost my best friend, and with her, I lost a part of myself.

The Pretence

The following day, Tanishka and I did not speak. It was as if we had both decided to pretend that our world hadn't tilted on its axis. When Avantika arrived, it felt surreal. We all got together as if nothing had happened, as if the previous day's emotional upheaval was all in our minds.

Tanishka appeared to have gotten over it; she smiled more broadly while talking to Mihir. I sat back and watched, a twinge of jealousy eating away at my insides. She was happier than I'd ever seen her, and I lost her through my own decisions. It twisted something inside me, the thought that I never made her feel valued enough.

I turned my focus to Avantika, determined to give my 100 per cent to our relationship. 'If can't be a good best friend, I can at least be the best boyfriend.' I just wanted a space where nothing could go wrong, and no one would get hurt. We spent time together, and for the most part, everything looked perfect. We laughed together, shared secrets and, for a while, I almost felt as if Tanishka was an old memory, slowly fading away.

However, as the days turned into weeks, the feeling of an eternal loss started haunting me. I missed Tanishka's laughter and the pearls of wisdom she offered, and how we could talk for hours. It was entertaining with Avantika, but I just felt like I was putting a bandage on a wound that needed more than temporary relief.

As we sat together in silence one afternoon, I finally spoke the words I had been mulling over. 'Avantika, can we make it official?'

Her expression changed as she paused and turned towards me. 'Dev, it's not the right time yet.'

I felt a familiar disappointment wash over me. 'Why not? It's uncomfortable to have everyone pretend that we're not more than just friends and that we're just friends, especially when we're not just friends.'

She shrugged, looking away from me. 'I just don't want to move too fast. We'll get there, I promise.'

An awkward silence stretched between us, the conversation left in the ether. Smiling despite the confusion and frustration boiling within. My life seemed complicated, entwined in the thread of feelings I had not fully unspooled.

As much as I tried to focus on us, I couldn't shake the thought that Tanishka was happy with Mihir, and that was the hardest pill to swallow.

My Breaking Point

I was trying to give my all to the relationship with Avantika. But as the saying goes, 'When you give someone your all, they start taking you for granted.' Everything seemed okay on the surface.

I still remember the day: 16 March. Avantika shared a PG with Tanishka, and I wasn't exactly keen on visiting all the time. One afternoon, Avantika told me she was on her period and asked if we could skip our usual meet-up. 'I'm really tired today, Dev. Can we please meet another time?'

I nodded, trying to mask my disappointment. 'It's fine. You rest. We can catch up later.'

After leaving, I decided to play badminton to clear my mind. As I walked, I called her to check if she needed anything, but there was no answer. I got her favourite cheese burst pizza to surprise her.

One hour passed with no word from her. I got worried, and decided I would go check on her. I knocked on her door, but no one answered. I could hear footsteps from inside, but then, there was silence. After fifteen minutes, Tanishka opened the door, slightly confused and looking a bit out of sorts. I could smell a hint of alcohol on her breath as she spoke.

'What's up?' she said, her annoyance evident in her tone. 'I had to see Avantika,' I said, fuming with annoyance. 'But she won't let me in.'

I could see Mihir in the background, and the sight stung. I had no right to question him or what was happening behind that closed door. 'Just let me see her,' I insisted, but Tanishka shook her head.

'She's sleeping. You can't go in.'

Then, out of nowhere, Avantika appeared in a black crop top, her lips painted in bold red lipstick and there was a spark in her eyes that suggested she hadn't been sleeping at all. My heart raced. 'What happened? Are you okay?' I asked.

She snapped angrily. 'I told you; I'm not seeing anyone today. Why are you here?'

Something shifted in her eyes, a defensive stance I had never seen before. She was looking past me, and I knew—someone else was there. I felt rage boil inside me, especially when Mihir said, *'Chal bhai,* let's go. Leave them alone.'

'Stay out of this, Mihir. It's my personal matter,' I shot back, my voice rising. I turned back to Avantika. 'Can I come in?'

She pulled my shirt to hold me back, desperation in her voice. 'No need. Just go.'

But I couldn't leave. My mind wouldn't let me. I pushed past her into the apartment, her grip on my shirt loosening. What met my eyes was a punch in the gut. There were two pizza boxes, a bottle of vodka on the table, and four chairs, which added up to another person behind closed doors.

I ran into the room where I had heard the footsteps, my heart pounding. And there he was, Mehul, one of the ugliest guys I had ever seen. It looked as if Avantika had asked him to hide. The sight of him was enough to boil my blood. Everything crashed around me, my mind drawing a complete blank.

I staggered back into the hall, anger and despair crashing together. I kicked the table as hard as I could, sending the pizza and vodka flying to the floor. The sound was thunderous, and for the briefest moment, I struggled between the panic-inducing blast of glass shards and a glittering rush of adrenaline. I could almost hear the laughing betrayal in that shattered silence.

I yanked Avantika by the hand and pulled her into the next room, slamming the door shut behind us. I was crying; she was stoic.

'Avantika, Why? What made you do this? You could have told me!'

She didn't cry. 'I didn't want to hurt you; I thought it would be easier this way.'

'Easier?' I repeated incredulously. 'You think this is easier? Do you even understand what you've done?'

I heard Tanishka, Mehul and Mihir pounding on the door, pleading, *'Bhai, khol!'*

'Why?' I yelled back, my voice raw with pain. 'Why would you do this to me?'

Avantika stood there, her expression a mix of guilt and fear. 'I thought you'd be angry; that's why I didn't tell you. I didn't want you to react like this and now, please, for God's sake, just go. *Aaj se sb khatam.*'

As she spoke, the weight of her words hit me like a freight train. My heart shattered; I could feel the ground underneath me giving way. 'And what about this?' I was shaking my arms, my hands grasping for air. 'What is this? You're not who I thought you were!'

I looked into her eyes, and, for a brief moment, I saw a flicker of the girl I had fallen for. But it was overshadowed by the pain and betrayal.

She opened the door, and as I turned to leave, I noticed the watch she had given me still on my wrist. In a moment of sheer frustration, I took it off and threw it at her, watching as it clattered to the floor.

'I don't want this,' I shouted, my voice echoing in the silence that followed.

'Dev, wait!' she called out, but I was already stepping away.

'Are you my boyfriend or what?' she said, her voice trembling in front of everyone. 'We're not dating, and you can't prove that we ever were.' I could see the confusion in their eyes, deepening the ache in my chest. She was trying to make it clear that she wasn't the one in the wrong, that she hadn't cheated on me. I noticed Tanishka standing there, looking hesitant, as if she wanted to speak up, but Mihir was subtly holding her back.

Mehul smirked, stepping forward. 'Dev, this behaviour is unacceptable. Who gave you the right? You think you can just storm in here?'

'Her mother won't tolerate this,' he continued dismissively. 'You think you can act like this and have no consequences?'

'*Maa ch***a, be******od,*' I snapped, my anger boiling over. I couldn't believe the audacity of his words. And with that, I turned on my heel and left the PG, the weight of everything crashing down on me.

As I stepped out, I felt defeated. my mind felt heavy with the weight of my losses. Everyone thought I was in the wrong; that I had messed up.

I lost everything in a moment—my best friend and my love. As I walked away, I glanced back at H3 304, the room where I had lost it all. It felt like I was leaving behind a part of myself, and the world was closing in around me.

The Day of Revelation

That was the day I finally understood why people drink, why they smoke, why they do anything to numb the pain. The ache inside was too much to bear. I needed an escape, a distraction—anything to keep my mind from spiralling deeper into the mess I was in.

I ended up at Pavni's place. When she opened the door, I saw a girl sitting on the couch with her. I was in no mood for introductions or small talk. In my head, I was like: *'Who the fuck is this?'* But I didn't really care to ask. I needed to speak to Pavni, and this random girl wasn't going to stop me.

'Pavni, I need to talk. Now.'

Her eyes opened wide, sensing the gravity in my tone. She rose, told her guest she'd be right back and took me out to the balcony. We weren't exactly best friends at that moment, but she was the only person I could rely on, who might be able to make sense of this madness with me. And, now? Now she is my bread and butter, the one constant in all this madness.

But that night, I didn't spill everything. I couldn't. The whole *Tanishka* thing was too raw, too complicated. So, I stuck to Avantika. I let it all out, how she'd made me feel like a fool, how she turned everything on me in front of everyone, acting like we had never been together. Pavni listened quietly, her face growing more shocked with every word.

'You've been dealing with this on your own?' Pavni asked, disbelief and a hint of anger creeping into her voice. 'Why the hell didn't you say something sooner?'

I shrugged my shoulders, trying to compose myself. Honestly? I wasn't prepared. I had no idea how to articulate this, how to explain this crazy mess that was now my life. Where does one even start? It was not just a breakup story; it was a messy network of betrayal, confusion and losing parts of oneself along the way.

'I don't know, Pavni,' I said quietly, staring at the distant lights of the city, my eyes averted from hers. 'I think . . . I didn't want to believe it was real. If you talk about it, it is real, you know?'

Pavni reclined back in her chair, crossing her arms, her brow furrowed in thought. 'Listen, Dev, I just gotta ask this . . . Do you think Avantika and Mehul had . . . you know . . . something going on? Or were they just . . . there?'

I exhaled. The thought had run through my mind uncountable times, yet it had a gut-punching effect when she said it out aloud. 'They might be. Why else would she hide all this from me?'

She raised an eyebrow 'Wohi toh, if it was not a thing, then this would all have been in the open.'

As Pavni and I were quietly speaking, the door to the balcony creaked open. I looked up—it was Palak, the uninvited guest, our classmate.

She dangled a cigarette from her lips in a way that reminded me of Avantika. I stared for a few seconds; the déjà vu hit me hard.

'How's it going, fellas?' she asked, interrupting the silence. 'All okay, Dev? You look a bit . . . off.'

Pavni's answer came forth quickly, maybe a bit too quickly. 'Nothing, Palak. Just some college stuff. Working on it.'

But Palak wasn't dumb. She looked at both of us, her eyes narrowing, like she knew something more was going on. Still, she didn't push it. She just took another drag from her cigarette, exhaling slowly.

I couldn't help but ask, *'Kya milta hai* cigarette *peeke?* What's the point?'

She blew out a stream of smoke and shrugged. *'Acha lagta hai bas.* Relaxing.'

For a second, I just stared at her, then I reached out, my hand open. 'Pass it.'

I took two, maybe three drags of the cigarette. The smoke hit my lungs, and for a brief moment, everything felt . . . lighter. My mind, which had been racing non-stop, started to slow down. It was strange—how something so small could calm the chaos.

Palak, leaning against the railing, flicked her cigarette. *'Bhai,* peg *khatam nahi karna?'* she asked Pavni, her tone casual but knowing.

Pavni turned to me. *'Tu piyega kya,* Dev?'

Without hesitation, I nodded. 'Yes.'

And that was it. One peg turned into five or six. As we slugged back drinks, the tension between us dissolved. We became closer the more we drank. Alcohol works wonders in transforming strangers into friends—by the fourth peg, it felt as if we had known each other intimately for years.

Somewhere between the fourth and fifth, I began to talk. Really talking. I told her everything—Avantika, Mehul, the whole mess. I spilled it all out to Palak and, this time, it felt not like a burden.

But Tanishka . . . She was like the last piece of chocolate, too valuable to share. Secrets, our promises. As drunk as I was, I could not talk about her. Some stuff remained buried, out of reach even through booze or talk.

Being Sidelined

I wasn't really enjoying Palak and Pavni's company anymore. I tried to laugh, tried to be present, but it felt hollow—like something was missing. Maybe it was Tanishka, or maybe Avantika. Hell, I wasn't even sure anymore.

Whenever I saw Tanishka and Mihir, it was like they were ripped out of some romantic drama—happy, glowing, perfect. I felt a hit of jealousy running through me. They were there on display, radiantly happy, while I felt like the neglected page of a book that had already been read. And then there was Avantika. She was inescapable for me. We were in the same class, and every time I saw her, she was glued to her phone, texting that bastard. I felt as though I had vanished into thin air and become a ghost watching from the sidelines.

Late-Night Calls

I was just trying to move on, trying to understand it all. Most of my nights were spent overthinking, lying on my back, staring at the ceiling, wondering how it had all gone wrong. On one of those late nights, my phone buzzed. I looked at the screen—Tanishka calling. Without any second thought, I picked up.

'Hi,' I said, my voice hardly a whisper.

'I can't really talk,' came the response, with a distant, almost hesitant-sounding voice. 'But . . . *tu thik hai?*'

I paused for a second, searching for words. 'Yeah . . . I mean, yeah, trying to make sense of it all.'

She sighed. *'Maine teko warn kra tha* . . . it was too early.'

There was no way around it. She had warned me, but it didn't lessen the pain at that moment.

'But *thik hai,*' she said gently, 'whatever happened, forget it and move on. Meet someone new.'

I couldn't stop myself. 'You have moved on, right? Glad with Mihir?'

On the other side, the momentary pause was followed by a response, one that soon sounded sharper than before. 'Much happier. At least I've someone who knows not to make me feel sidelined.'

'*Haan?*' I couldn't help but mutter as something tightened painfully in my chest. 'Then . . . why this call?'

She hesitated a bit and then sort of softened. 'You were my friend once . . . and I just wanted to know whether you were okay.'

I took a deep breath, forcing a smile she couldn't see. 'Okay.'

When the call finished, I sat there staring at the phone. '*You were my friend once,*' her voice played over and over in my ears.

Were. As in the past. It hit harder than I expected.

I stood by the window, watching the city lights. Everyone else had moved on, but I was still here—stuck between memories and what could've been, trapped in the silence where the past refuses to fade.

I reached for the pack of cigarettes on the table—Palak's influence, I guess. I didn't even like smoking, but that night, it seemed like the right thing to do. I lit one and inhaled deeply, the smoke filling my lungs and, for a moment, the ache in my chest dulled.

I wanted to call someone. Pavni, maybe. Or even Palak. But it didn't feel right. They weren't part of this story. Not the real one, the one buried deep beneath all the casual conversations and late-night drinking sessions. The one I couldn't share with anyone.

I thought to myself that Tanishka was right. I needed to move on. I needed to let go of whatever I was holding on to. But how? How do you just erase memories, shared moments of everything that once mattered so much?

Searching for Closure

Days passed, and I felt caged . . . in one never-ending loop. I would walk into the class, and there she was—Avantika: on her phone, laughing and chatting away. I was sure it was Mehul she was talking to, and that thought twisted inside me like a knife. Try as I might to distract myself with thoughts other than her, but she was simply impossible to forget. It was a reminder of all that I had lost and of what she had chosen instead. I was looking for answers, and I needed them fast.

I couldn't keep living like this. I needed closure—proper closure. If I was ever going to move on, I needed answers. Why did she cheat? What went wrong? Was it I? Did I do something?

I opened WhatsApp, scrolling through my contacts until I found her name. Her chat wasn't at the top anymore; it felt like ages since we'd spoken. But I took a deep breath and typed out a message: 'Can we meet once?'

Seconds felt like hours as I waited for her reply. 'For what?' she asked.

'*Ek baar* . . . or you want to make this a scene like you did at my PG?' she again messaged

131

'Just wanna meet. No drama,' I sent back.

After a moment, she responded, 'Last time?'

'Yeah,' I replied. 'My place?'

'Fine,' she said.

Fifteen minutes later, she arrived. Avantika walked in, and as she sat on the bed, I settled into the chair across from her. It felt strange—last time, we'd lounged together, everything so intimate and comfortable. Now, we were miles apart, both physically and emotionally.

'Why did you call me here, Dev?' Avantika broke the silence, her voice tense.

I took a breath. 'Just tell me why, Avantika. Why did you cheat?'

'Do you think I cheated?' she shot back, defensively.

'Then why were you hiding Mehul?' I pressed, trying to keep my cool.

She looked away, frustration evident. 'I knew you would react. That was the main reason I didn't want to tell you. And I promised Tanishka, I wouldn't mention it.'

'Why didn't you accept that we were dating in front of everyone?' I asked, my heart racing.

'Because Mehul was there!' she exclaimed, her eyes finally meeting mine. 'If he saw us together, he'd tell my mom, and I didn't want to create any mess. You know how she is. He came to say goodbye since he's going back to college, so we were partying.'

I felt a surge of anger mixed with confusion. 'So, you chose to hide everything instead?'

She shifted uncomfortably. 'You always seemed off with Mehul. And for me, I can't just leave him.

He's my ex, but we've known each other since class 3, I can't break my friendship with him,' she admitted, her voice barely above a whisper.

My mind was struggling to digest this. 'But what should I do with all of this? Am I just supposed to accept it?'

I looked at her, my mind racing. 'Are you telling the truth? Swear on me.'

She held my gaze, calm and composed. 'Yes, Dev. I'm not lying. Don't you trust me?'

I stared at her, trying to find the truth in her words, but everything felt so tangled.

I sat there, torn. Should I believe her? Could I trust her words after everything that had happened?

'Then why were you always talking to Mehul in class? Every time I looked, it was like you were glued to your phone, chatting with him.'

She sighed, almost annoyed now. 'I wasn't always talking to Mehul. I was talking to Sneha . . . I was sharing everything with her. Yeah, sometimes I talk to Mehul too, but not always. It's not what you think.'

The room fell into an awkward silence, heavy with the weight of unresolved feelings. My heart was torn between wanting to believe her and the anger that still lingered. I couldn't shake the doubts.

Before I could respond, she leaned in suddenly and kissed me. It caught me off guard, and for a second, everything else disappeared. The confusion, the hurt, the questions—it all melted away in that moment.

If I think about it now, girls always have that card to play—something they can use to erase their mistakes. It's like a secret weapon they can pull out when things get messy, and guys often just fall for it, forgetting everything else in an instant.

After that moment, I looked at her and said, 'Please, *aage se kuch mat chupana.*' I needed honesty— no more secrets.

If I look back now, I realized I was also cheating— emotionally, at least, Avantika had no clue about Tanishka; that we were best friends at one point, or why I had suddenly stopped talking to her.

Lost in Illusions

Days passed, and things gradually started healing between Avantika and me. We were together, but a part of me still couldn't fully accept it. Maybe that's what love does to people—it makes you do things you never thought you would.

Sab sahi lag raha tha, like everything was falling into place, but I knew deep down I was living in some kind of illusion. We were together, and as time went on, I found myself forgetting about Tanishka—at least trying to.

People often use something to heal their pain; maybe I was using Avantika to forget Tanishka. One distraction to replace another.

I was always insecure with Avantika, especially when she talked to Mehul. It was like a constant knot in my stomach that wouldn't go away. Even though we were together, the shadow of him always lingered, making me question everything.

When I shared all this with Palak and Pavni, they didn't hold back.

'Dev, *pyar mein log andhe hote hain, aur tu c****ya ho gaya hai,*' Palak said, shaking her head.

Pavni chimed in, laughing, '*Sahi bol rahi hai yeh. Tumhe khud bhi nahi pata kya chal raha hai.*'

The Summer Internship

The last year of college also brought the long-awaited summer internships when one steps out of the four walls of a classroom and into the world outside. It was perhaps the most defining phase—the phase in which each one of us had to step out of the comforting arms of the campus to prove ourselves worthy in the eyes of the real occupational world.

Everyone went away for an internship, to different posts, different cities—the geographical spread, of course, included the rest of the country. Avantika and I were also given separate determined locations. She got Rajasthan, which coincidentally was where Mehul also lived. But I couldn't say anything, could I? I wanted to ask her if she had chosen it for that reason, but instead, I kept quiet. Everyone was excited about their internship placements. Amidst this, my mind wandered to Tanishka. How was she faring? Where was she posted? I wished to know, but it never seemed to be the proper timing. Hardly did we ever communicate. Each of our conversations now barely consisted of reported exchanges about collegiate work.

Even that felt stilted as if loads of things had been piled up between us that we were both purposely ignoring.

Amid the buzz of internship placements, I spotted Tanishka standing alone in the corner. Some glow of hers was missing; she appeared withdrawn, far-off, defective, as if a stone was upon her. It reflected somehow, she wasn't as happy as she used to be.

I wanted to ask if everything was fine. But for a variety of reasons, I did not. Avoiding the growing awkwardness between the two of us just seemed so much better. During the days until the commencement of the internship, I could not shake off that something was terribly, terribly wrong.

At last, just before we went off to our internships, I spotted her sitting alone in the campus courtyard scrolling through her phone. That very minute was my chance.

'Is everything fine?' I asked, trying to sound casual, hoping she'd open up.

She replied with a simple, 'Yes.' Her tone was vague, and it was clear she wasn't interested in building any more conversation. I guess she didn't want to share, or maybe I wasn't the person she wanted to talk to anymore.

As silence hung between us, I turned away, realizing the distance between us had only grown. I couldn't help but wonder—was it too late to fix this, or had we both moved too far apart to ever go back?

And I chose to just exit quietly.

Summer Break

As the summer break began, we both left for our respective internships. Avantika and I talked regularly, but our conversations were more routine—about work, daily life and how we were managing. Everything felt smooth between us, almost too smooth. It was as if the complications of the past were fading away, and I found myself gradually forgetting about Tanishka.

One night, when I was on a call with Avantika, my phone suddenly vibrated. I glanced down and saw Tanishka's name flash on the screen. Without thinking, I quickly told Avantika, 'Papa *ka* call *aa raha hai,*' even though I knew that wasn't true. I wasn't sure why I felt the need to hide it from her, but I did.

I called Tanishka back, and she answered, '*Agar tu* busy *hai, toh baad mein* call *karti hu.*' I felt a rush of happiness just to hear her voice. '*Nahi, bta! Kya haal hai? Kaisi hai tu?*' I asked eagerly.

'*Sab theek hai,*' she replied, but her tone was neutral.

We started catching up, asking each other about our lives, how everything was going and where she was interning. It felt so good to reconnect, and I found myself wishing it could last longer.

Finally, I asked, '*Aaj achanak aise kyun* call *kiya?*'
'*Bas aise hi,*' she replied.

After this small talk, we wrapped up the call. The moment I hung up, I was engulfed by an uncomfortable feeling that almost seemed as if she, too, missed our friendship. Having something left unexpressed in the air—a sort of feeling that she wanted to say something very important, but I didn't want to press her for anything. Still, the thought lingered in my mind about what she hadn't shared.

To soothe my conscience, I texted her: 'Is everything okay? Everything all right?'

Her reply came short: 'Yes.'

'*Kal baat karte hain.* Good night!' I typed back, hoping for more but resigning to her silence.

The next day dragged on, sitting in the office staring at the full quant sheets, each hour appeared to be dragging longer than the last one. Numbers pranced about as if they were mocking me. What was I even doing here? I was never good at maths!

At last, night descended, and I decided to act boldly and call Tanishka.

After some small banter, I asked, 'Is there something on your mind? I know we're not as close as we used to be, but if you want to share, I'm here.'

There was a brief silence before she spoke, 'It's just . . . Mihir has changed completely. He treats me like an object. I'm just here when he needs something. He prioritizes his friends, and I feel like I don't even matter. He brushes me off whenever I try to talk and just asks me to hang out with my friends instead. It was not like this before. I used to mean something to him, but right now I feel invisible.'

My heart sank at her words. 'Why are you still with him?' I asked, struggling to understand.

'Because I love him,' she replied, her voice wavering.

Again, she said, 'You haven't left Avantika yet, have you?'

'You're right,' I said, feeling the weight of her words. I wondered how love could make you do anything, even prioritize someone else over yourself. It was as if love often blinded you to your own worth.

'Why didn't you tell me all this earlier?' I asked, my voice barely above a whisper.

'I didn't want to jeopardize my relationship,' she confessed. 'Mihir dislikes you, and you know how insecure he was during my birthday.'

The knife twisted in my chest: 'Is Mihir this important now?'

'You are doing the same thing. You chose Avantika over a friendship with me.'

Her words struck home, and I saw the irony in both our situations.

In hindsight, looking at those events, both of us were suffering from the same issue; no one was happy, except for Avantika and Mihir.

The Weight of Choices

Days of our internship passed, and Avantika was as busy as an ant. I'd call her and she would just brush me off with a *'baad mein baat karti hu, busy hu'* or wouldn't take my calls. I was fed up with the routine that day and asked carelessly, 'Are you going to meet Mehul?'

She hesitated for a moment, 'Maybe . . . but I don't know.'

Her vague, evasive response sat in the air, and a familiar ache set in. It was like a reminder that when she wasn't there and out of my sight, she didn't care or love me anymore. She was far away, and it made all things feel eerily different, like we were in separate worlds.

And then, as if on autopilot, I found myself calling Tanishka. It just felt like talking to her happened in a smooth flow—no pressure, no drama. After all, we were just friends, and besides, she was in a relationship too. Our conversations flowed naturally. We laughed about silly things, gossiped about teachers and even mocked our classmates' terrible fashion sense. At one point, we realized Avantika and Mihir were practically twins—both experts in drama.

Two months passed by like a blur, happiness fleeting as it always is. On the second-to-last day of our internship, Tanishka dropped the bomb.

'Basu, now when we go back to college, we won't be able to talk like we are doing right now,' she said, her voice trembling over the phone.

A lump formed in my throat. 'Why? Is Mihir really so important to you?'

She paused for a moment, as if trying to find the right words. 'I can't really afford to lose him. He is already so insecure about you! I just . . . I don't know how to keep the balance.'

'So, you're actually going to let him decide with whom you can be friends?' I asked, my frustration just under the surface.

'That's not it!' she protested, her voice rising. 'I really care about you, but Mihir needs me! I am still willing to be friends, just not the same way as before—more like acquaintances.'

I shook my head, although she couldn't see it. Her words cut more than I'd imagined. 'You're doing the same thing I did with Avantika: choosing love over friendship. How did we get here?'

'I didn't want it to come to this,' she replied, her voice trembling. 'But things have changed. I don't want to hurt Mihir. You know he'll create a scene if he finds out I'm talking to you. I just can't do it. It's like he's become my priority now, and I can't risk that, I'm sorry.'

At that moment, I felt an overwhelming rush of emotions. Suddenly, I cut the call, unable to bear the weight of her words any longer. It hit me like a wave—I realized this wasn't the same Tanishka I once knew, the one who had given me a TED talk about love in moderation.

Now, she was treading the same path I had feared, and jealousy clawed at me like a relentless beast. It was clear—Mihir had taken my place in her life, and I was just a lane she'd turn to when she needed comfort.

Return to Reality

As the internship drew to a close, I headed back to college, but this time I felt no thrill. The world into which I was stepping felt like something I had already escaped. Back when things were in the online mode because of COVID, life had its share of troubles, yes, but at least I knew what to expect.

I texted Avantika that I would be reaching by 4 p.m. She had arrived earlier that day; probably all set up and ready to rush into college life since morning. I thought she would want to meet up, so I added a casual *'milte hai?'* to my message, hoping for a warm response.

As soon as I landed, I switched off the flight mode. One of the notifications was from Avantika: *'Haan.'* That was it. No more explanation, no excitement. Felt a bit like déjà vu; the familiar feeling of uncertainty crept back in, like some old movie playing again.

Determined to make the best of things, I stopped at a nearby shop and picked up chocolates and a bouquet of flowers. A small gesture from my side to reawaken our moment before life gets all swirly.

Back at the PG, I texted Avantika to tell her that I had arrived. 'We can meet whenever you're free,'

I said, keeping it light yet hopeful. After about twenty minutes, my phone buzzed with her reply: 'Okay.'

When she finally walked into my room, I grabbed her by the waist, pulling her close as I whispered, 'Hi, Miss Khargosh.' That nickname always brought a smile to her face. I leaned in, rubbing my nose gently against hers in a way that only we understood.

With her still in my arms, I slid her to the study table and reached for the gift I had gotten—some chocolates and flowers. 'For you, my Khargosh,' I said softly, watching her reaction.

She smiled, taking the gifts from me, 'Thank you!'

But something in me wanted more than just polite thanks. I leaned in closer, my fingers tracing the curve of her waist, my voice dropping to a teasing whisper. '*Itna* busy *thi tu? Time nahi mil raha tha mere liye bhi?*'

She sighed, brushing a strand of hair behind her ear in a way that always drove me a little crazy. '*Nahi, kaam tha* office *mein yaar samjha kar,*' she replied, her voice softer now, but distant. Then, with a small, mischievous smile, she added, '*Ab bas* college *ke* last six months *bache hain.*'

I smirked, pulling her even closer. '*Ab bas* college *ke* last six months *bache hain or bas kuch nahi, sirf tum aur main . . . aur bahut saara* sex,' I whispered, as my lips drew close to hers.

She giggled, playfully pushing me back. '*Haan nikal ja, kisi aur se le le.*' Her eyes teased me, sparkling with flirtation.

But I didn't let go My hands around her waist somehow tightened themselves as I locked her close against my chest.

'*Itni hot bandi ke hote hue, kisi aur ke paas kyun jaun?*' I murmured into her ear, my breath brushing against her skin.

Her teasing demeanour faded for a second as she looked into my eyes. '*Mere se ummid mat rakh.*'

Taking that as my cue

I drew her closer. In that very second, with a steady, slow movement of my thumb on her cheek, I began my kiss. The kiss was soft and, in a way, we had all the time in the world to relish it. Her laughter, slowly fading, found space in the rhythm of the heartbeat as our breaths became rhythmic. Crossing her arms around my waist, she crawled towards me, getting so close that the kiss deepened and turned more passionate. It was, however, not merely physical; it felt like we had lost each other, basking in a kind of warmth neither of us wanted to let go of.

With that, I picked her up and carried her towards the bed, and as if it was second nature, her legs wrapped around me like clockwork, our breaths mingling for a moment before I realized she had encompassed me in the sheets. The outside world ceased to exist for a moment.

As my lips traced their way down her neck, I felt her shiver beneath me, her breath catching with every kiss. Her skin was soft, warm and intoxicating. I moved lower, my lips exploring, savouring every inch. But as I reached just below her ear, my lips brushing the side of her neck, I froze.

A mark—small, faint, but unmistakable—a hickey.

My heart skipped; my breath stilled. I pulled back slightly, my eyes fixed on it, the warmth between us suddenly shifting. For a moment, I stared, my thoughts racing as a thousand questions swirled in my mind.

As I pulled back, trying to make sense of what I was seeing, I straightened up and stared at her. Before I could say anything, Avantika, sensing my hesitation, asked, 'Kya hua?'

Without thinking, I blurted out, 'Yeh hickey kisne diya, Avantika?'

She looked at me, eyes wide, then burst out laughing, trying to brush it off. 'Pagal hai kya tu? Kya bol raha hai? Arey, koi kirde ne kata hoga ya kuch mark hogaya hoga,' she replied, waving it off casually.

I wasn't buying it. 'Itna bhi ch***ya nahi hu ki hickey aur kirde ke kaatne ka difference nahi pata chalega.'

She smirked, rolling her eyes. 'Kirde ne kata hai, sach mein!'

I stood there, my fists clenched, unable to let it go. 'It's Mehul, isn't it? That's why you've been distant, why you've been too busy for me.'

She looked at me, her face hardening. 'Are you serious right now? Tumhara dimaag kharab ho gaya hai? You're just making things up.'

'I'm not blind, Avantika! You've been avoiding me for weeks, ignoring my calls. And now . . . this? This mark?' I pointed at her neck, my voice rising with each word. 'Don't tell me it's nothing.'

'Shut up, Dev!' she whispered, hurrying to face the door. 'You don't have the freaking right to shout at me like this!'

'Then explain it to me! Why him? Why did you do it?' My heart raced; there was anger and hurt, pooling in every limb within me.

My voice rose again. 'And you think I'm stupid? It's him, right? Mehul! You've been avoiding me because of him, right? Busy with "office work"? You've been lying to me all along!'

'*Pagal ho gaye ho tum!*' she shot back, her eyes narrowing. 'You don't know what you're saying!'

'Don't I?' I yelled louder, stepping closer. 'Stop lying! You think I don't see it? You've been with him, haven't you? That's why you've been so distant!'

And then, just like that—smack!—her open palm slapped hard against my face. It could have knocked me over. It was shocking; the very force of the slap stung my cheek and had me stumbling a step back.

She looked at me, her eyes burning with fury. 'How dare you!' she screamed. '*Tumhe koi haq nahi hai mujhpe awaaz uthaneka!* You think I owe you an explanation? You think by shouting at me you have some power over me?'

I stood there with my cheek on fire, my mind racing. I couldn't believe it. She slapped me. Anger mixed with hurt, and my thoughts were heavy with confusion.

Clenching my fists, I spoke, 'Why Avantika? What made you lie? What made you do this to me?'

Her voice felt cold, flat. '*Jo sochna hai, socho.* I don't care. *Bas.* I'm done with this, done with you.'

And with that, she left, leaving me without the slightest clue to satisfy my burning curiosity. The sound of the door slamming rang out through the dead air of the room; I was still reeling from the stinging slap on my face.

Still in shock, I turned towards the mirror buried in the wall.

How exactly did we find ourselves here?

How on earth could I let it go this far? Was I so blind? The collective load of everything struck me at once—her walking away, the silence between us and the mess that I had created.

I stared hard at myself, choking on reality. I had lost her. Maybe long before tonight.

Funny how the ones who say they'll never hurt you . . . always do.

I grabbed my phone and called Pavni and Palak, needing someone to talk to. They arrived quickly, looking concerned but curious. As we settled down, I took a deep breath and shared the whole messy story with them. As I narrated it, tears came rolling down my eyes.

I took a deep drag from the cigarette I had lit, trying to calm my racing thoughts, but the tears started spilling over.

'Seriously, *kya tumhe lagta hai wo iss drame ke layak hai?*' Palak added, concern creeping into her voice as she watched me struggle.

Pavni, sitting beside her, shook her head, her expression softening. '*Bilkul! Humne toh kaha tha ki wo ladki hi ch****a hai. Tum uske paas kyun gaye phir?*'

Her playful tone couldn't mask the genuine worry etched on her face.

'*Chal, ro mat,*' Palak said softly, reaching out to comfort me. '*Aise ch****a ladkiyon ke liye kyun rone laga hai? Tum* better deserve *karte ho.*'

'*Sun,* your CAT paper is on 27 November! Now, leave all this and concentrate on studies,' Pavni ordered affectionately.

Their words echoed in my mind like a painful reminder of what I chose to do, and soon, tears streamed down my face as I came to understand just how deep a mess I had gotten myself into.

Pavni added, 'Exactly! Read and study more for a change. You have got your exams coming up and you need to go all-out.'

'*Chal, hum chalte hain.* Give yourself a little time,' Pavni said, getting up.

'*Bhai, sab theek ho jayega,*' Palak told me as they both got ready to leave.

'Thanks, guys,' I said, torn between gratefulness and despair.

Echoes of the Unsaid

Days followed their monotonous course, and each lecture produced whips of emotions that hit me. There she was, right before me, video calling her friend and her staccato laughter reverberating in my ears like a demoniacal tune. I felt as though she were taunting me, akin to a cat toying with a mouse. Amidst the agony of not being able to focus on any thoughts, my eyes fixated on her—a magnetic pull amidst confusion and pain.

Sometimes I even questioned myself. *Kya meri galti thi? Uski thi?* All I knew was that instead of an apology, I received a stark slap of reality—she had gotten over me, and I was left behind like a shattered piece, struggling to stand upright.

My mind became foggy, and when the time for the exam approached, I couldn't even study. All I could do was relive those moments with Avantika, trying to explore whether she had ever cared or not.

It was ridiculous. I wanted to share all these thoughts with Tanishka, but she seemed so absorbed in her so-called love story.

Shattered Focus

October came along with its chill, but it felt strangely empty. We had not spoken—no messages, no casual hellos, nothing. As if we were a pair of ghosts ignoring each other's presence even though we shared the same space. I was trying to focus on gearing up for the exams, drowning in quant problems that were nothing less than a nightmare for me.

They say that time is the ultimate healer; time doesn't erase the pain; it teaches you how to live with it. I wondered if that was right. Every day, I mumbled a sense of acceptance to myself, however distorted it was.

In the midst of all this, I found relief in unexpected places. Believe it or not, I developed an unbelievable knack for smoking. An absurd coping mechanism, I know, but at least it kept me distracted.

Pavni and Palak were my constant and steadfast companions; forming the bane of my existence. Despite their boyfriends being a pain in the ass sometimes, they always kept me entertained

One day, while we were all together, I teased them.

'Honestly, I think these boyfriends of yours create more of a problem than they are worth,' I said, smirking. *'Tum logon ka taste to mere se bhi kharab hai.'*

Pavni rolled her eyes and laughed, *'Haan, isiliye aaj tu yahan baith ke apne* decisions regret *kar raha hai.'*

Palak chimed in, 'Exactly! *Aur hum dono khud ke liye bhi tumhari tarah* regret *nahi kar rahe! Tumhare* taste *ka kya kehna bhai!'*

I laughed, but their words struck a chord. My heart was finding it difficult to forget Tanishka; after all, she was the only one who knew more about me than anyone else.

Even as I tried to keep my spirits up with my friends, the absence of Tanishka felt like a void I couldn't fill.

The Return

Then came 14 October again, like an uninvited, quiet reminder. This year was different. People whom I had counted on, filling every corner of my life in the past two years, started receding into oblivion. Friends were there—Pavni, Palak and others—but the ones I really wanted next to me were no more.

Pavni and Palak had organized a grand surprise birthday party for me. They set up my place to bring some vigour and energy, but I was not finding it exciting, just another day—just another reminiscence of how things had changed.

Just after 11:55 p.m., someone knocked on the door. Palak stood up and opened the door, and I heard a familiar voice. My heart stopped. As I walked into the hall towards the door, I saw her—*Tanishka*.

She looked just as she always did, standing there frozen in time. But before I could think of anything else, I saw him too—Mihir, sitting there on his so-called bike waiting to drop her off. He didn't spare a word for me; he just cast me a glance and drove away without a single look back.

I closed the door and turned around. I just couldn't believe she was here. 'You're here?' were the words that popped out of my mouth without any thought.

She teased, her voice light. *'Kya? Maine jau phir?'*

I quickly said, *'Nahi re, matlab* how?'

Tanishka brushed it off, *'Ye sab chhod,* cake *kaat le pehle ya gate pe hi mujhe sab puchna hai?'*

We all laughed and gathered around as I cut the cake. After the celebrations, Tanishka handed me a gift—a sleek HRX jacket. This jacket easily became the most precious thing in my wardrobe. Not that I don't own expensive stuff, but this . . . this is different. It means something more.

After a few rounds of funny banter with everyone, I pulled Tanishka aside to the balcony. *'Tu kaise aayi?'* I asked, genuinely curious.

She smirked, *'Arrey, tujhe khushi nahi hai toh main chali jaati hoon.'*

'Arey *pagal, aisa thodi hai,'* I quickly responded.

'Mihir ne kuch nahi bola?' I asked, knowing how things had been between them.

She sighed, *'Do ghante jhagra karke aayi hoon.* I had to convince him that I had to be here tonight.'

Then she began sharing the whole story—what happened between them, the arguments, the reasons—everything. We stood there, the cool night breeze brushing against us.

And I gave her a friendly hug and thanked her for coming. I really wanted her to be there. I told her, *'Apne* boyfriend *ko smjha de* ch****a *hai wo.'*

She laughed, giving me a light punch on the arm. *'Chup ho ja,'* she muttered, but I could see the relief in her eyes, like she needed this too.

After that, we all laughed, our drinks in hand, the room filled with the kind of carefree chaos that only comes when everyone's high on alcohol. People were cracking jokes, making fun of one another and, for a while, it felt like everything was just . . . easy.

Around 4 a.m., there was a knock on the door. Tanishka's ride had arrived. Mihir. He was here to pick her up.

She waved bye to everyone, a half-smile on her face, saying her byes before slipping out the door. The laughter in the room lingered, but there was something about her leaving that left a void, at least for me.

As the door clicked shut behind her, I leaned back, staring at the ceiling, lost in thought. That day, I realized something—Tanishka and I would always be friends. No matter what happened, no matter who came or went, I wasn't going to let her go.

But . . . I chuckled to myself.

'Bas, iske liye Mihir ko jaan se maarna padega, kyuki ye ladki iske pyaar mein bilkul pagal ho gayi hai.'

Waiting on the Inevitable

College life would soon be coming to an end; only four months were left for the final leg of the journey to be completed. The focus had begun to shift from studies to personal development, placements and other distractions. Classes had now turned into a facilitating procedure, with everybody busy trying to get a job or somehow complete the last lap. Lectures had become backdrops of the fun and excitement, which was all about the future—interviews, CVs and, of course, the ever-existing pressure of figuring out 'what next'.

In the middle of all this hype and hysteria, I surprisingly found myself to be very chill. The results were out, and I scored 91.90 in my CAT. This was what one would call a curse broken for a general candidate in today's hyper-competitive world. The best part was I did it on my first attempt! Not that I had any great expectations, but my enthusiasm on the verge of tasting success and admission to a good college was almost palpable.

Everyone congratulated me, except Avantika.

As I walked along the campus, I felt a surge of gratitude towards Tanishka. She stood by me during my summer internship break by lending me money for my form when I was dead broke. I returned the favour a few weeks later, but I had yet to give her the credit she deserved. So, I decided to take her for a choccy to show my little token of thanks.

The lines of our conversations had been reduced to occasional 'hellos' when passing each other in the corridors, yet I wanted her to know that what she had done for me really meant a lot.

I found myself wishing for Mihir and Tanishka's breakup once college was over. I knew it was wrong to hope for someone else's relationship to end, but I had always blamed that bastard for the distance between Tanishka and me.

The Final Countdown

I worked my way through lots of interviews for different institutes in the next few months. I was on a mission to find the one best fit for me. The PR cells of some colleges were doing their work splendidly, going on about how great everything was, including mind-blowing placement packages.

After managing to speak with a few alumni and having been exposed to real experiences, I made my future decision: I accepted the offer letter from IIM Goa.

With that achievement landed, the bitter reality of my undergraduate days came to an end. The days slowly dwindled, and we counted them down, as though it were a countdown to a lift-off. 'Only five days left!' I would yell to my friends, who would roll their eyes and laugh at my dramatics. 'Four more days!' I would scream the next day, the kinetic energy in the air could be felt.

The countdown had hit zero, and it was goodbye day. It was a bittersweet moment, the day we graduated from college—a culmination of laughter, tears and memories formed among comrades. We were all dressed for a party to honour this unforgettable ride, but deep down, I knew a new ride was set in motion.

Today, my legs felt shaky as I approached Avantika. I took a deep breath and asked, 'May we talk for a second?' She nodded, a little quizzically.

'Why? You have to tell me today,' I pressed, trying to keep the tone light while my heart swelled in tune with a racing motor.

'Yeah, It was Mehul,' she said, taking a long sigh, 'and seriously, it was just that one time.'

I looked at her, a mix of emotions swirling inside me. 'I'll remember you for a lifetime,' I said, my voice steady. 'You taught me that love shouldn't be blind. Because of you, I learned to keep my eyes open.'

As the weight of the past hung in the air between us, I added, 'And thanks to you, I found my best friend.'

I nodded, feeling a sense of closure wash over me. With that, I turned and walked away, leaving behind the remnants of a relationship that had taught me so much. As I stepped into the fresh air, I felt lighter, ready to embrace whatever came next.

Old Rhythms, New Realities

After college ended, we were trying to get out of our comfort zones to start a new life outside college. As my college was supposed to commence in June, I took a break by taking a trip for a few days.

One day, with nostalgia and hope in my heart, I called Tanishka, praying she would say she had broken up with Mihir.

'Hi, Basu! *Kya haal hai?*' she said sweetly.

We fell into our old rhythm, as if we had been getting together every day since college. Sharing memories and updating each other on life made my spirit soar. It all came rushing back all of a sudden, and for a fleeting moment, I forgot about the whirlwind.

After a few minutes of normal chatter, I finally found the courage to ask, 'So are you two still dating?'

'Yeah, we are,' she answered, much lighter than expected.

It was as if I could feel she was still crazy about him, but I didn't want to push it. I understood she would rather leave that topic alone, perhaps uncomfortable with it, perhaps because I was not significant enough for her to share those things with me anymore. Thereafter, we talked about good old college days, reminiscing and laughing over so many memories, as if there had been nothing at all that had changed between us. But deep down, I knew something had.

As days passed, the duration of our calls kept increasing. I was free, and so was she, and it felt like we were slipping back into the easy rhythm we used to have. But every now and then, when Mihir called her while we were on the phone, she'd cut my call immediately. It was clear who was more important.

I didn't say a word about it, though. I just went along with it, reminding myself that I was just her friend now.

IIM Goa

And after weeks of waiting, June finally rolled in, and there I was—Goa. I was about to join the Indian Institute of Management Goa. Sounds crazy, right? I mean, who wouldn't be excited about this? IIM, new beginnings—it all felt like a dream.

But within two months, that dream crashed hard. I realized . . . I was in hell.

Hell, because this campus ran on just three hours of sleep—enough to survive the next twenty-one hours of madness. Friendship? Nah, it was all about forming diplomatic connections, carefully choosing your circle, because everyone was playing the long game. And if you were seen hanging out with someone of the opposite gender, rumours flew faster than campus Wi-Fi—people would jump to conclusions like, 'Oh, they must be hooking up!'

But the real punch? That twenty lakh we all invested? Yeah, not for the learning or the professors. Nope. It was for one thing and one thing only—placements. Everyone was there for that golden ticket. As for the professors? If you dared to ask them to review your paper, they'd just look at you and say, 'Stop cribbing.'

And those exams? Ah, the midterms. You'd get the results of your last midterm . . . during the next midterm. Efficiency at its best.

It was a campus where the teachers had less power than the students—or those infamous 'cells' running everything.

I was one of the youngest in my class. And the subjects? . . . They felt like a throwback to school, as if I was sitting in standards 1–10 all over again— mugging up facts without a clue. Critical thinking? Who needs that when you can just memorize everything, right?

But they took 'discipline' seriously—only when it came to students, of course. If you were even a second late to the exam hall . . . Bam! You're out. No second chances! But when meetings were supposed to start at 9 and the authorities strolled in at 9:45? 'Oh, that's totally cool!'

They had a proper smoking zone—like, wow, what an achievement! But if that zone got too crowded? No worries at all! Just light one up in your room with the doors closed. Discipline at its finest, right?

A place where toxicity reached its peak, where everyone was competing against everyone else, whether in class or for placement—there was no escaping the rat race!

Then there was relative marking—oh joy! If your peers scored just one mark higher than you did— guess what? Your grades took a nosedive. It was like being stuck in a never-ending game of 'Who Can Stress More?'

My Escape from the Chaos of MBA

Amid all this chaos, I found myself sacrificing an hour of sleep to talk to Tanishka—the girl who brought my energy back. We spoke regularly, and even though Mihir was in her life, who cared? I was getting what I needed from those conversations. Just having her in my life made me genuinely happy.

That one hour felt like magic. It wasn't about me pouring out my entire day; it was her sharing hers. She'd start off with, *'Tujhe pata hai, Basu, aaj kya hua?'* And it could be anything—a kid showing up on her floor, followed by his frantic mom searching for him.

I listened to her with rapt attention, wide awake and plugged in while she told me the most boring yet entertaining stories. Every word felt like a warm hug in the middle of a storm. No matter what was happening in my world of deadlines and tests, only for that moment, I let the world slip into oblivion, losing sense and meaning, with the sound of Tanishka's laughter lending magic to our connection.

When Friends Become Confidants

Every day, my morning *officially* began with Tanishka's 'good morning' text—around 10 a.m., of course—she figured anything before 10 was still part of last night.

Days passed by in a blur, and we grew closer. From her side, it was becoming more than just casual chats. As for me? I had always been close, at least as a friend. I still remember, she was the first person I called when I cracked IIM Goa. That moment felt big, but what felt even bigger was how she started sharing things she held close to her heart—stuff she wouldn't tell just anyone. The way she shared with me, it reminded me of the bond we used to have, and all I wanted was to get back to that place we had before, the one I felt I had lost.

I guess this was the moment I could finally ask about Mihir. So, one night, during our usual call, I casually brought it up.

'So, how's everything going with Mihir? You guys doing okay?'

She sighed, 'Where does he even have the time? We barely talk anymore. He's either at the gym or stuck in the office, and by the time night rolls around, he's already asleep by 10. He doesn't even call me . . .'

I decided to press a little more, the typical best friend question creeping in. *'Tujhe dikhta kya hai usme?'*

She paused before responding, a teasing tone in her voice. *'Woh achha hai, kam se kam aaj tak toh mujhe cheat nahi kiya.'* She was clearly teasing me about Avantika.

Then she added, 'But there's only one thing I don't like—he's very dominating.'

'What do you mean?' I asked.

She started sharing everything about Mihir—his dominating nature, the way he treated her and how he was super possessive about everything. Yet, she also mentioned that, deep down, he did care for her in his own way.

I asked her, *'Toh* why don't you leave him?' She replied, 'I'm just waiting for things to get better. We're trying to sort things out.'

I started to realize that she seemed to be over-investing in him while he didn't even seem to value her. It felt like she was dating someone who was always too busy for her, and it made me realize that Mihir was often too caught up in his own world to appreciate what he had.

Closer than Ever, Farther than Before

At this point, our conversations were completely unfiltered. We could talk about anything—her family, the annoying boyfriend or the daily random madness. Nothing was off-limits, and that level of comfort made everything so much easier.

That has always been my expectation from Tanishka—to have a raw, flat talk; no pretences, just the real us.

Once, one night, during long confinement in our usual late-night chats, I posed her the question, 'Can we be best friends again?' With a teasing smile, she said, 'Yeah, but only if Avantika doesn't come back into your life!'

I asked for just one promise, a small one—'No matter who comes or who goes, we don't break this bond. If you ever feel it slipping, just look a little closer . . . don't let us fade.'

And she assured, with promise. 'I am not gonna break this.'

This was all I ever wanted—a best friend in my life. But, as they say, once you get what you want, you start expecting more.

Day by day, talking to Tanishka became my habit. It was like my morning coffee—essential, energizing and, sometimes, a little too much. But as much as I enjoyed our conversations, I couldn't help but wonder if getting too close was harmful. I started thinking that maybe this habit was turning into something I couldn't live without.

However, Tanishka was in a totally different boat, trying to keep her relationship afloat while I was secretly wishing it would hit an iceberg. It's not that I wasn't happy seeing her happy; I just couldn't stand that guy. She deserved better—much better than the one she was dating.

The Mistake of Regular Conversations

Now, every day, Mihir would do something ridiculous, and I'd have to listen to the entire story. Tanishka, of course, would narrate it like the latest episode of a soap opera.

'*Basu, tujhe pata hai aaj kya kiya Mihir ne?*'—and then I'd get the full episode.

It became a regular thing—me, sitting there like her unpaid therapist, while she described Mihir's latest antics. Honestly, it felt like I was stuck in a never-ending sitcom where Mihir played the lead, and I was the unfortunate audience who didn't even sign up for the show.

Days passed by, and the toxicity between Tanishka and Mihir kept increasing. Long-distance relationships were already difficult, but with Mihir? No distance was far enough to escape his controlling attitude. He kept telling Tanishka that her habits had to change: he seemed to want to shape her, control her—a traditionalist, domineering kind of guy who thought everything should go his way.

Whom she could goddamn follow on Instagram, which goddamn pictures she was allowed to post.

That one night we were on a call, and I could feel that something was not right. She was quieter than usual. I asked her what the problem was, but she waved it off at first. It was only when I asked her for the fifth time that she really broke down sobbing over the phone.

I didn't even need to ask. Mihir! Same reason she had cried so many times before.

Without flinching, I said, 'Leave him, Tanishka. *Uski shakal se leke akal tak kuch theek nahi hai.* You can do much better, *yaar.* Better to let him go.'

I was silent for a moment and then added, 'Wait a minute—wasn't it you who gave me that whole TED talk on what love in moderation means? What happened to that, huh? Please, dude, do you really think you deserve this? C'mon, Tanishka, you're much better than some guy who treats you like this.'

She spoke softly and tremulously. 'I want to. But . . . *nahi ho pa raha hai.* I need time to leave him. It's not that easy.'

The line went silent and, for a moment, I could feel her inside that silence.

Sensing the heaviness in her voice, I quickly tried to switch the conversation, hoping to lighten the mood. '*Chal,* let's talk about something else.'

'By the way, did you finally watch that new show I recommended, or are you still stuck on your so-called boring cartoon . . . oh wait, sorry, your "beloved" anime series?' I teased, throwing in a bit of sarcasm to make her smile.

Nothing seemed to work at first; she was still lost in her thoughts. But, after some effort, after throwing in a few more jokes and teasing her about her anime obsession, I finally managed to bring a little smile to her face. It wasn't much, but at that moment, it felt like a win.

Engineering Chaos and Birthday Blues

Here I was, battling every subject and every professor, just praying for this term to end. I mean, I couldn't stand another engineering subject! Like seriously, these engineers with their obsession over numbers and equations—if solving alien maths problems was their thing, why didn't they just stick to their engineering labs? What are they even doing here in an MBA—writing love letters to calculus?

Finally, after surviving eight brutal exams—two per day—I scribbled my way through the end of term.

I walked into my first class of the second term, thinking, 'Finally, a fresh start!' And what do I see on the board? QAM, an operations subject—full of x, y, alpha, beta, sigma!

Seriously, it felt like they were running some secret boot camp for engineers.

I somehow survived four more lectures, each professor more confusing than the previous. By the end of the week, I realized I was wrong about the second semester being easier. With more engineering subjects and more alien maths, I still had no clue what 'sigma' actually meant.

Amid all this academic chaos, the most consistent part of my life was listening to Tanishka rant about Mihir's latest acts of possessiveness and controlling behaviour. It had officially become part of my routine—engineering subjects by day and Mihir's 'greatest hits' by night.

Then, October crept in quietly. My birthday month. Honestly, I don't know what beef God has with my birthday. Every year, it's either the best or the worst thing—no in-between. And the only way to figure out which one it is? Well, you've got to survive the whole year just to know.

I had enough surprises, though. I thought to myself, for the last three years, it felt like something chaotic happened every October. So, here's to 2023: Please, just be good to me.

As October rolled in, companies buzzed into the campus like bees to honey, clipboard in hand and checklists at the ready.

After doing over a hundred iterations of our resumes, everyone on the campus was hoping for the shortlists, but let's be real—it was all a game of luck until you sat for that personal interview. Each company had its own set of absurdities; some wanted to maintain gender ratios and would only shortlist female candidates, while others seemed to have mysterious criteria that only they understood.

But I found no company that was actually looking for candidates who could perform T-tests with pen and paper. Instead, I was left wondering if my skills in

Excel and PowerPoint would ever see the light of day in this madness.

Amidst this chaos, I got a notification on my phone: 'Your parcel has been delivered.' Confused, I blinked at the screen. I hadn't ordered anything. My curiosity was piqued; I made my way to the parcel collection area.

When I opened the package in my room, I was greeted by a bottle of perfume and some skincare products. Yes, I was the kind of guy who dabbled in a five-step skincare routine, but only a select few knew about it. My thoughts drifted to Pavni and Palak; those two clowns had never even given me a free pen, so where on earth did this come from?

It didn't take long to connect the dots. Without a second thought, I snapped a picture of the gift and sent it to Tanishka with a quick thank you.

'Thought you might be expecting a watch, right?' she replied.

'Why's that?' I asked, genuinely curious.

'You don't remember Avantika's line?' she teased. 'When she gifted you that watch, she had said, "If you give someone a watch, you're also giving them a piece of your time."'

I replied, '*Yaad aaya*.'

'Absolutely,' she shot back, 'but I think she was just keeping track of how much time you wasted on her.'

I couldn't help but smile at her teasing. The playful banter was exactly what I needed to cut through the stressful week.

Here I was, drowning in company rejections and October chaos, yet Tanishka somehow knew how to make things feel light-hearted again.

A Birthday Bash and Breaking News

Three days of impatience, and finally, it was my birthday! As I readied myself for the frenzy that typically accompanied this day, I prayed, 'No surprises this year, God. Please.' But, well, God being God, I had no expectation of favours.

At midnight, my phone buzzed. It was Tanishka, sending birthday wishes, her voice bright and cheery.

I marked my birthday with a good, old-fashioned boys' night out, during which there were a whole lot of punches. The boys loved me in their own special way, which was to beat the crap out of me. No questions asked.

The party raged on, fuelled by copious amounts of alcohol and cigarettes. By 3 a.m., I was officially *'bhand'*, completely out of it. As my friends started to drift away, they made sure to give me one last round of good wishes before heading off. That's when I got another call from Tanishka.

'How's the birthday going?' she asked, but her voice was dull, lacking its usual sparkle.

By now, I could tell something was off. I had known her long enough to sense it in her tone that this call was about something serious. 'What's up? Just spill it, please. I'm not really in the zone right now,' I urged, sensing the weight in her words.

'I broke up with Mihir,' she said, and my world stopped for a second.

'What the fuck!' I exclaimed, the shock hitting me like a ton of bricks. I mean, part of me felt this exhilarating rush of happiness for her; she deserved so much better. But another part of me was in a spin. Yesterday, everything was fine—what the hell happened?

My mind raced to catch up. 'What? How?' I managed to ask; my voice was soft, almost a whisper.

She began to cry and that was the instant my buzz began to wear off. I had never heard Tanishka weep quite like this in my life. There was a real pain in her voice, a depth of sorrow that broke through my drunken haze. I could feel her heart breaking on the other end of the line, and it was like a punch to my gut. Suddenly, my birthday didn't feel like a celebration anymore.

'Please, *yaar, chup ho ja.* Just tell me what happened. Please, don't cry,' I begged, trying to stay coherent while my head swirled with alcohol and confusion.

I wasn't accustomed to seeing her like this— so broken and vulnerable. With every sob of hers, I became more concerned, and my heart sank further. She had been the strong one, the one who kept things together.

Finally, after an eternity, she felt like talking. And when the words came tumbling out, it was so much worse than I could have ever imagined. Mihir had said something so vile, so revolting, that I couldn't even bear to repeat it. The kind of thing that made my skin crawl just from hearing it second-hand. It was that despicable.

No man with a shred of decency would say something like that—not to a stranger, and certainly not to someone he claimed to care about. The fact that she had to hear those words from someone she loved made it all the more horrifying.

'Tanishka, listen to me,' I said, my voice firm, almost cold. 'If you ever speak to that guy again, I swear I won't talk to you either. Not once. This isn't love, it's poison.'

There was silence on the other end. I could hear her breathing, her thoughts spinning in the quiet. I didn't know if my words would change anything, but I had to try.

After a pause, she finally said, 'No, I won't talk to him anymore.'

'Good,' I replied, my voice firmer now. 'If you've got even a shred of self-respect left, don't ever speak to him again.'

She stopped crying, a quiet resolve in her voice. 'I won't,' she promised.

I sighed, relieved but still upset. 'Just think, Tanishka. Because of him, how many people have you lost? For two years, you didn't even talk to me on campus because he didn't like it. And it wasn't just me—he had issues with every guy you interacted with.'

There was silence on the other end, but I could tell my words were sinking in. I had to push her a little further, though.

'Please, end this chapter. Your exams are coming up next month, and you need to focus on that. Give your 100 per cent. I know it's hard, but you *can* move on. Last year, I was in your shoes when Avantika cheated on me, but I had to pull myself together. Right now, your career is what matters most. Prioritize that.'

After another fifteen minutes of talking, her mood started to lighten. I could hear a faint smile in her voice, and the weight of the conversation began to lift, if only a little.

'*Kal baat karu?*' I said, easing the conversation to a close. But before hanging up, something tugged at me.

'*Ek baat aur kahoon?*' I hesitated for a second, unsure if I should go on.

'*Haan, bol na,*' she replied softly.

I took a deep breath. '*Aaj tak maine kabhi bola nahi,* but you deserve so much better than this, Tanishka. You deserve the kind of love that doesn't make you cry, that lifts you up, not tears you apart. You deserve the world, and all the happiness that comes with it.'

Her silence urged me on. 'You deserve someone who looks at you like you are their everything, because you are. Someone who makes you feel like you're more than enough, not someone who makes you question your worth. And honestly, I just want you to know . . . if anyone ever makes you feel less than that, they don't deserve *you.*'

The line was quiet for a moment, but I could feel the emotion between us, hanging there, unspoken yet palpable.

Then, she spoke softly, her voice almost a whisper, 'Thank you.'

After that, I hung up the call, feeling a mix of relief and concern for Tanishka. I checked my phone, hoping for some distraction, and found a notification from Avantika: 'Happy birthday, Dev'.

I paused for a moment, contemplating whether to reply or just let it be. In the end, I typed back a simple 'Thank you.'

But as I stared at the screen, my mind drifted to deeper thoughts. *Is physical cheating more painful, or is it the emotional betrayal that truly breaks you?* It's like asking which cuts deeper—the knife or the words that follow.

Physical cheating? Sure, it hurts, leaves some bruises and brings in some seething frustration deep down, but eventually, those feelings lose their ground. Now, as for emotional betrayal . . . that's something else! It just haunts you! It is an echo around you that makes you question everything that you are. Was I not good enough? Did I miss the signs?

It's not merely loss of love; it's a loss of self-esteem—for you're drowning in a sea of self-doubt that appears inescapable.

I had experienced this with Avantika; now I saw Tanishka suffering the same anguish of emotional betrayal, her suffering a reflection of my own scars.

'It's easier to heal than to rebuild trust.' Apparently, one leaves scars, while the other leaves doubts.

'Beh****d,' I murmured as I settled onto the bed. 'Oh God! At least, let me have one normal birthday. I am unable to take so many shots every year!'

Saying this, I fell into sleep, hoping against hope for a semblance of normalcy.

Healing Together

Slowly but surely, things began to shift. Tanishka was healing day by day, and I was right there, making everything possible for her. Each laugh we shared and each late-night conversation lifted her spirits just a little higher. The dark clouds were parting, revealing the sun that had long been hidden.

Our bond blossomed into something beautiful. We could talk about anything—family problems, dreams, fears—nothing felt off-limits.

It got to the point where if I didn't hear her say goodnight, I couldn't sleep. We talked so much that her voice became essential to my nights.

But with every passing day, it gnawed at me. I was becoming closer to Tanishka and something had me questioning, Was this friendship even real? It felt like a lot more. I didn't want to overthink it, but I felt like this was just crossing the borders of friendship.

Why did it feel like I was getting so attached? Maybe it was those late-night last messages?

I kept on telling myself that I should consider her just a friend, yet every laughter and every moment seemed to pull us closer together like the weaving of a blanket that kept us warm.

What would I do with this though? I wanted to make sure I would not ruin what we had; however, I could not ignore the way my heart would race when she laughed. There was this mixed thrill and fear.

Slowly, a change was happening. As the months rolled on, my attitude towards Tanishka started undergoing subtle changes. The light-hearted friendship began to slowly dissipate on my end, morphing into something deeper, a lot more complex. The questions I intended to ask were not the ones a friend would—they were layered, filled with implications that I myself couldn't quite grasp.

The late-night conversations didn't feel light anymore; they felt weighted, like each word was testing the boundaries of what we were. Friendship? It didn't feel like that anymore. Now, everything felt like a countdown to something more, something unspoken.

It was as if I was searching for something beyond friendship, even though I wasn't ready to admit it. When she laughed, it wasn't just her laughter I heard—it was the way my heart reacted, skipping a beat, betraying what I had been trying to suppress.

The Social Service Bomb

And just like that, my third term was wrapping up. Before I could even think about catching a breath, the college decided to drop the bomb. Apparently, after taking twenty lakh rupees in tuition, they figured, 'Why not send these kids to do some free labour in the name of giving back to society?'

I opened the email with a sense of dread. A month of social service? Alright, let's see where they were shipping us off to. Scrolling through the Excel sheet, my eyes stopped at my name. Rajasthan. I couldn't help but laugh at the sheer ridiculousness of it all. Out of all the places in the country, they had to send me there.

But wait, it got better. Along with my golden ticket to the desert, there was a team list: Vaibhav, Tanmay, Prashoon and Kaustubh. A solid mix of workaholics, alcoholics and, well, the occasional free rider. Just perfect.

And the mission? Stopping tiger poaching in Ranthambore. Yeah, because who better to solve a wildlife crisis than a bunch of overworked MBA students? I mean, we were supposedly experts in critical thinking, right? But when I thought about it, our version of critical thinking seemed to boil down to something much simpler: just asking ChatGPT, 'What's the best way to save tigers? And can you break it down into bullet points, please?'

When I shared my plans with Tanishka, she burst out laughing. 'Ranthambore? That's near Haridwar, right?'

I couldn't help but think, 'How does she know the Indian map better than I do?'

'Yeah, I guess so!' I replied, trying to sound confident.

I grinned, 'So, we can totally meet up then!'

She nodded, '*Haan, mil sakte hain!*'

The only problem was how to convince my team to let me leave for a few days to meet Tanishka. I could already picture the conversation: 'Hey, guys, I know we're supposed to be the tiger saviours of Ranthambore, but I've got a more pressing matter—like hanging out with Tanishka. So, if you could just hold the poachers here while I go rescue my social life, that'd be great!'

I could already picture their shocked faces as they processed the idea of me ditching them to meet a girl, trying to explain that to a bunch of guys who thought 'friend' meant 'potential girlfriend'. I'd have to somehow convince them that it was totally normal to prioritize friendship over saving the tigers.

When we landed in Ranthambore, I quickly realized something: Rajasthan had some pretty decent people. Which led me to one simple conclusion— Avantika? Definitely, a factory defect. I mean, how can an entire state be filled with nice folks, and yet she's the one glitch?

Anyway, our reporting officer kindly informed us we had a meeting scheduled for the next day. In this scorching heat? Fantastic. Naturally, we needed a solution. That's when Kaustubh came up with the most logical conclusion: beer. It was the perfect antidote to being roasted alive.

So, we grabbed a few bottles and settled in for the evening. Well, except for Tanmay—the token guy in every group who thinks cold drinks and snacks are as thrilling as life gets. He was probably off sipping Coke somewhere, and we didn't say a word because, honestly, he was the only real workaholic among us. The rest? Free riders or alcoholics,

But my real challenge was figuring out how to sneak out early without making it seem like I was ditching tiger-saving duty for something a bit more important.

After a few rounds, I decided it was time to drop the bomb. 'Guys, listen, I need to head out the day after tomorrow. I'm meeting up with Tanishka.'

A stunned silence fell over the group. Then the laughter erupted.

'Wait, so *tu yahan* project *chhod ke ek ladki se milne ja raha hai?*' Kaustubh exclaimed, wide-eyed.

'*Ladki ka chakkar, babu bhaiya!*' Vaibhav chimed in, winking like he'd just solved a mystery.

Prashoon—*jiski zaban se zyada sakal kaali thi*—couldn't resist throwing in his two cents. '*Bhai, tujhe* sex *nahi milega! Tu mat jaa, woh* periods *mein hogi, dekh lena!'* he said, shaking his head as if I'd just committed the ultimate crime against humanity.

I couldn't help but think, *Kya bolu in sabko?*

Somehow, they were all convinced—it must be the magic of alcohol. Well, except for Tanmay, the sober one in the group. The Coke-sipping legend had been uncharacteristically quiet, staring at me with the cold drink bottle in hand, silently judging my life choices. *A Perfect example of maintaining diplomacy.*

The Morning After

The night before, standing at the station, I clutched my train ticket like it was perhaps the golden ticket to a new adventure; I got off at Haridwar at six in the morning—greeted by the calm beauty of the place—and a cab took me to Tanishka's apartment. Excitement began to bubble within me.

As I stepped out of the cab, my eyes lit up as I saw her waiting for me; and in that moment, the world faded away. Tanishka looked stunning in a light pink nightdress, one that shone softly in the morning light. And let me tell you, it was less 'friendly vibes' and more of 'you might need a life jacket for this wave of feelings!' We hugged on one side, and warmth rushed through my body.

'*Itni subah ki hi train mili thi*,' said Tanishka, her voice soft and heavy with sleepiness, a smile curling upon them.

'*Arey, me agaya milne wo kafi nahi hai kya?*' I tried to keep it light.

Once we entered the apartment, she looked at me and said, 'I am going to sleep for a while. You go into the other room and sleep.'

'*Wah,* this is quite a treatment!' I said to myself, both amused and honoured with the casual invitation.

As her voice faded into the background, I opened my laptop and got to work. I needed to wrap up everything so Tanmay wouldn't have any complaints.

Conversations and Confessions

It was 10 a.m. now and a gentle knock came at my door. Tanishka stood there, now slightly more awake, mischief dancing in her eyes.

We spent the morning catching up; I told her all about how I ended up convincing my team to let me even come here.

She talked about her B-school interviews—apparently, a nightmare involving corporate jargon—and an interviewer who looked like he hadn't slept in days. We even did a little post-mortem on Mihir, with the mutual conclusion that he was, in fact, a certified *ch***ya*. Though, I could still sense a part of her that hadn't fully let go of him, a little flicker of something deep down.

After that, we decided to step out for a bit and headed to her so-called favourite restaurant—Kalsang Café. She had hyped it up so much, but when we bit into the momos, the disappointment hit harder than I expected. '*Yeh toh* hostel *ke mess wale* momos *jaise taste kar rahe hain,*' I joked, and she laughed, but even she couldn't defend them. So much for that recommendation!

After the tragic momo incident, we grabbed some beers and headed back to her place for a low-key Netflix and chill session.

After a long discussion about which movie to watch, we were stuck between her obsession with anime and my love for SRK. But after a bit of back-and-forth, we settled on something we both could tolerate—*The Conjuring*. Horror and beer—perfect combo!

We stretched out on her bed, sharing a blanket as we leaned back, heads resting against the wall, our legs stretched out in front of us We cracked open the cans and, with the cold fizz bubbling up, the room was comfortably dim, with just enough light from the TV flickering across her face. She was fully engrossed in the film, and I also got lost—not in the film, but in her.

We sat side by side, occasionally sipping our beers. I tried to focus on the movie, but all I could think about was her—sitting right next to me, so close yet so far from where I wanted her to be. She looked so relaxed, but my heart was racing faster than it had any right to, given that *The Conjuring* wasn't exactly terrifying me.

I was thinking about what I really wanted to tell her—what I had been holding back for so long.

My heart raced faster than the spooky soundtrack. Should I just blurt it out? Tell her how I actually feel?

The movie was halfway through, but I couldn't hold it in any longer. I took a deep breath, my heart racing, and I decided to ask.

I looked over at her, my voice low. '*Ek baat bolu?*'

She paused, the can of beer at her lips, and looked at me. *'Haan, bol na,'* she said, sipping as though it didn't matter. But for me, this moment felt monumental.

'Tanishka we are not on the same page,' my words stumbled out.

There was no dramatic *I love you*, no grand declaration. It was simpler, more honest. Just like how she had told me once . . .

I had fallen for her, and now it was out there.

She stared at me for a moment, then set her beer down on the table, her expression soft but serious.

'Dev, this time . . . there was no *Basu*, just Dev,' she said quietly, like she was piecing her thoughts together. *'Kya hogaya aisa?'*

I felt a lump in my throat, but I knew I had to be honest. 'I don't see you as just a friend anymore. You're not just someone I care about; you're becoming my everything,' I confessed, my heart racing as the words left my mouth.

She sighed, the smile still lingering but fading quickly. *'Abhi* . . . I can't see anything, Dev. I can't build trust again,' she replied, her voice barely above a whisper.

For the first time, I actually understood something behind the alcohol in her eyes—more of herself than a reflection, really. Her voice fell soft and broken to fill the silence: 'There is still something . . . for Mihir . . . I do not know what it is, but there is something.'

I could see she was struggling through the pain of it all; her eyes glimmered, and one could say they included things more than just booze. She misspoke, trembling in a voice just a whisper above the fetid silence: 'But I don't want to face anyone like that. Sometimes I feel just useless and lost altogether.'

Tears began to well up in her eyes, and I felt something twist in my chest. Without thinking, I reached out to hug her lightly, to let her feel the mere warmth of my being there for her.

'You are not worthless,' I said gently, the weight of her emotion lay heavy on both of us. 'You are an irreplaceable addition to someone's world.'

She stayed there for a moment as her breath quieted, as though my words wafted warmth into an opening her soul didn't know it needed.

With unsteady fingers, she brushed the hair away from her face and looked straight into my eyes, her voice slightly trembling: '*Hum . . . bas dost rehte hain na?*' The desperation in the statement held the softest whimper in it.

'If you don't want *dosti*, Dev, we can cut it out. I know this feeling you have, but I'm sorry . . .' She looked away, blinking rapidly, trying to hold it together. 'I know you've helped me a lot, but . . . *maine ab uss* way *mein nahi dekhti hoon.* I'm really sorry.'

Her voice became thick with emotion with the last few words, and I saw the guilt and conflict in her eyes. She was not just saying no—she was caught between what she knew and what she felt. She was obviously not ready for this, or for us.

I took a deep breath and smiled gently. 'It's totally okay. Let's just go back to how we were. I need you in my life, with no tag or label on it,' I said, calm in voice but not at all in heart.

She looked at me for a moment, her eyes searching mine, then reached gently for my hand and took it. 'Thank you for understanding,' she said in a whisper, her fingers chillingly tight against mine, as though saying so much more than words ever could.

I squeezed her hand back, trying to lighten the moment. *'Aur ye* "worthless" *ka* weightage *lekar mat ghoom,'* I said with a smirk, 'you're far too important for that.'

After that, we drank the beer, the movie still playing in the background, but neither of us cared. We were starting to feel buzzed. She began talking about Mihir, the one person I hated most. She shared everything—how much he had broken her, how deeply it hurt. I could see her eyes welling up again as she spoke, each word weighed down with pain.

I hugged her gently, this time wiping away her tears, just like she had done for me during the whole Avantika mess.

After that, something happened that couldn't be described in words—a moment that blurred the lines between friendship and something deeper. It wasn't planned, it wasn't forced; it just . . . happened.

It happened again.

Boundaries

I had one more day left in Haridwar, and as much as I cherished the moments we spent together, it was becoming increasingly clear that staying 'just friends' was going to be a struggle. I could see it in Tanishka's eyes; she hadn't completely moved on from Mihir. No matter how many times I tried to pull her away from those memories, it felt like she was anchored to them, a ship lost at sea.

'Tanishka,' I said as we sat on her balcony, the city lights twinkling below us. 'You're so much more than your past. Don't let him define your worth.'

Her eyes glistened with tears. '*Mujhe nahi pata, Dev. Kabhi kabhi lagta hai ki main kuch bhi nahi hoon.*'

I brushed the stray hair behind her ear. 'That's not true. You're beautiful and smart. Don't let Mihir's mistakes affect how you see yourself.'

We talked for hours, sharing stories, laughter. Despite the underlying tension, those two days flew by in a blur of comfort and companionship. But as the clock ticked closer to my departure, a heaviness settled in my chest. I didn't want to leave.

When it was time to undergo the ceremony of goodbyes, Tanishka stood transfixed by the door, her face reading something between gratefulness and something I could not fully pinpoint. 'Dev, I am really glad you made it, but please, let's keep our distance. I don't wish to move beyond friendship,' she murmured.

Her words threw me back in complete despair. 'I get that,' I said, forcing a smile. 'But it is very difficult for me to consider you purely a friend. You mean so much to me.'

She moved closer, her gaze fixed on me. 'Dev, I want to stay friends. I am not ready for anything more.'

'Okay,' I replied but the weight of her request was bearing down on me. 'I won't go against your wishes. But remember, I will always stand by you.'

As I walked away, I felt a bittersweet ache in my heart. Tanishka was right. A distance was needed between us. But still, somewhere deep down, I knew I was already quite far beyond the boundary.

Summer Reflections

I said my goodbye, half-sweet and half-bitter, and flew off to get the internship in Mumbai. The city came alive, and every evening I called Tanishka as soon as I returned from work.

Our conversations ranged from work complaints to campus gossip. Tanishka would dish on her latest devotions, and I would listen intently, always trying to be the pillow that she could lean her emotional burden on. But, in the back of my mind, I knew I was somehow more, but she never did.

One evening, Tanishka casually mentioned, 'Mihir called me today.' Her tone was somewhat annoying. 'I picked up, but . . . but it didn't feel the same as before. He was trying to manipulate me all over again.'

I was seething with rage. 'You need to totally dump him out of your life. Just tell him it's all over, don't even pick up his calls,' I said to comfort her.

'I did tell him,' she said quietly. 'I told him "I don't want to hear from you again." It was liberating, but . . . it still hurts.'

I figured she was beginning to heal slowly; she had an almost platonic perspective of our relationship. It hurt, but I tried to shove the feeling aside for now.

At about 3 a.m. one morning, my phone bleeped and woke me up. It was Tanishka.

'Dev,' she said, her voice ringing with excitement, 'I got accepted into St Xavier's for my MBA!'

My heart raced. I think that I was the first person she wanted to tell this news to. 'Wow, that's amazing! I'm so proud of you!' I gasped, flooding with joy for her.

'Thank you! I couldn't wait to tell you,' she said, and I could hear the smile in her voice. At that moment, it all seemed so right; felt like we had a great chemistry, without even crossing the limits we had for each other.

A Day Too Short

It was the last week of my internship. During one of our usual calls, Tanishka casually mentioned, 'I'm coming to Mumbai to meet my sister before heading off to B-school. I really need a vacation.'

I felt a surge of happiness. *'Mil sakte hain phir?'* I asked, hoping to see her one more time before everything changed.

She paused for a moment. 'But won't your internship be over by then?' she replied.

'Woh sab chhodo, tu bas aaja,' I said, my voice laced with excitement. I could already picture us meeting again, like old times. But in her tone, I sensed she wasn't as eager as I was.

Still, the thought of seeing her made me happy. She was coming a week after my internship was ending and even though my work would be done, I told myself I'd wait an extra week—just to meet her for a few hours. Men do such things in love.

The day came, and we met at the mall, a place that felt far too ordinary for a moment that meant so much to me. When I saw her sitting there, I couldn't keep my emotions in check. She looked like the most beautiful girl in the world—effortlessly stunning. My heart raced in a way it never had with Avantika. 'When you meet the right person, everything feels different. It's like you finally understand why nothing ever worked out before.' That's what it felt like with her.

I handed her a handwritten card, every word an attempt to convey just how important she still was to me. I also gave her a box of her favourite chocolates, hoping it might take her back to a time when everything felt simpler, sweeter. She smiled politely, offering me a cute key ring in return—thoughtful.

After a few minutes of banal conversation, we decided to watch a film. It was an ordinary decision, but somehow, in that dimly lit theatre, I wanted to touch her hand. It was absurd; I knew that. She was nothing more than a friend. Still, I wanted to take her hand and feel her fingers locked with mine. I took a moment and then slowly reached out. Then she gently took her hand off mine. It was neither abrupt nor rude—only a soft, subtle gesture; but it meant much more than any words could. She was still standing firm in the realm of friendship, while I had crossed a line I should not have.

After the film, she had to go. I offered to book a cab, knowing that this might be the last time I see her for years. All the time, I stared at the minutes tick away, trying to ignore how I felt as if a rock was settling into my chest. But when I looked at her, I knew for sure she did not feel that way.

As she got into the cab, a quiet sadness emerged. I tried to shake it, but the thought lingered. Maybe this meeting was not what she had wanted at all. The truth slammed into me just like a gut punch—perhaps, I had been asking for a little bit too much, letting my emotions confuse me as to what was actually going on between us.

'Expectation is the root of all heartache,' they say. I watched her cab disappear into the distance. Maybe, just maybe, I had been hoping for something she was never ready to give.

And the hardest part? I had waited an entire week in Mumbai just for these five fleeting hours.

Shifting Tides

I could see that our conversations were evolving—or devolving—as the weeks went by. What had formerly been effortless or normal conversation now seemed tense or forced, full of unsaid feelings. I was asking questions that blurred the lines of our friendship. 'How important am I in your life?' I asked, half-joking but serious.

A break ensued with an indication of hesitation in her. The laughter that had marked our conversation past a few minutes recessed, letting polite smiles and vague responses fill the void. Tanishka no longer seemed fully there, and I could feel the whole weight of expectation closing in on me.

Once cherished, it turned upside down, yet we did not lose our friendship. I was craving to preserve that friendship, even as I started finding myself in turmoil with the complications arising from my growing feelings.

Back to Campus

With the completion of my internship, I got back to the campus as a senior now. Such a rich atmosphere, with everyone's eyes glued on the juniors, resembling kids in a candy store. The gender ratio in our class was a disaster, and it seemed as if each guy had taken it upon himself to scout for newcomers in the junior batch.

Classes had taken a turn. It was not about mugging up the theories and definitions anymore; now it was the time for critical thinking and, more importantly, understanding the very workings of a business. It was no longer about pouring over 'case-*wase*' studies or textbook answers, as the professors expected and gave more weightage to the thought processes and the ability to solve real-world problems.

Tanishka was also about to join St Xavier's B-school and we still talked regularly over the phone. I supplied her with little bits of advice, like how to assign workload, deal with professors or find balance in the chaos. She would sit there and listen patiently, giving me an eye roll now and then, but I could always sense that little smile of hers surfacing on the other end.

The atmosphere on campus was both chaotic and strangely comforting.

Fading Conversations

After a few days, Tanishka eventually entered the new B-school life at St Xavier's. She spoke to me regularly, as she settled into the day-to-day assignments and the all-too-familiar toxic culture that's common within B-schools. But things had begun to change. Those long, easy conversations we would fill our time with slowly shrunk and, with each passing day, our calls grew shorter.

At first, I didn't pay much attention. I was aware that adjusting to a new college was overwhelming and she had a lot on her plate. After a few days, it was clear that something had changed. Whenever I called, it felt like she was in a hurry to end the conversation, as if there was an unspoken rush to hang up.

One night, after another half-hearted conversation, I finally asked, *'Tujhe baat nahi karni hai toh bol de, hum roj baat nahi karte hai.'*

She paused, and I could hear her taking a breath. 'Manage *nahi kar pa rahi hoon.* It's just ... everything's so hectic. *Hafte mein ek-do din baat kar lete hai, theek hai?'*

It hit me hard. This was the same girl for whom I would gladly lose sleep, just to talk for an hour longer. I used to treasure those conversations. Now, it felt like I was an obligation, something to tick off her list.

I just nodded and said, 'Okay.'

Once Close, Now Far

The mornings felt painfully quiet now—no more 'good morning' texts from her, no little moments that made the day feel lighter. Whenever I messaged her, the reply would come hours later, cold and distant, as if she were replying out of obligation, not care.

The nights were worse. My mind became a battlefield of unspoken words, of memories that now felt more like ghosts haunting the silence.

I couldn't help but ask myself—was it because I had confessed my feelings? Or, was it something else? Back when she needed someone to help her move on from Mihir, I was there, a constant, the one she leaned on. Now that she was happy again, moving forward with her life, maybe she didn't need me anymore. Maybe I was just a chapter she was ready to close, a part of her past she no longer wanted to carry. And the cruellest part of it all? I would have stayed, even as a forgotten page, just to feel like I was still somewhere in her story.

It hit me then—priorities aren't about having time; they're about making time. I used to make time for her, no matter how busy life got. But maybe, for her, I was a priority only when she had no one else, when her days were free and when she needed someone to listen to her.

And every night, I would be hanging on to that phone, waiting for her call, staring into that useless piece of technology, hoping that one unspoken promise would be fulfilled. But the calls never came. Not anymore. The silence on the other end felt heavier than I remembered.

Alternatively, sometimes I couldn't bear the silence anymore, and I'd go texting her. 'Busy?' and hope for a longish reply, something that would close up the growing rift between us. But the reply was short and dismissive, 'Yeah, just a little busy.'

And this time, this was not only a nightly affair, but it was leaking into my days as well. Be it sitting in class pretending to focus, or trying to get lost in something else, the thought of her absence would hit me—relentlessly.

I would find myself stuck in a loop of waiting—waiting for her texts, waiting for her calls, just waiting for anything to make me feel like I still mattered in some small way. But nothing came.

I was in for a long spell of waiting. Yet, when I would see her name flash on my screen, it would not pump life into my system anymore. Conversational dialogues that once flowed naturally now seemed stilted, forced and half-hearted.

A Call in the Night

It had become some sort of unspoken rule in our cluster—every weekend, no matter how chaotic our MBA life got, we'd party. Because what better way to handle the pressure of endless assignments, presentations and exams than drowning them in cheap rum and bad decisions? This was one of those nights, where we celebrated surviving another week. The music was loud and the drinks flowed—everyone was just trying to pretend that life wasn't as exhausting as it was.

Everyone was cracking one of their usual over-the-top jokes, and I was trying to blend in, holding a half-empty glass, when my phone buzzed on the table. I glanced down and saw *Tam* flashing on the screen.

For a moment, I could not figure out how I was supposed to feel. No thrill, no adrenaline rush—just the heaviness of what had once come easily or naturally. I apologized for leaving as I walked out to my room while forgetting about my drink in the noisy room.

I plopped down on the edge of my bed and stared at the phone for a bit before answering the call.

'Hey,' I said, steadying my voice devoid of the warm feeling experienced before.

'Free *hai?*' she asked.

'*Haan*,' I replied.

I tried to make small talk, '*Kya chal raha hai?*' I asked.

She sighed for a moment and said, '*Bahut kaam hai* college *mein*. Placement cell has kept a meeting at five in the morning.' She kept talking about how B-schools revolve around placements, the toxic culture and how exhausting it had all become. I sat and listened, letting her vent. I knew what it felt like; I had been there just a year ago.

'*Tana maarte hue,*' I said, '*Mujhe yaad hai,* I was in the same shoes. But *maine* time *nikaal ke baat karta tha roz*. Manage *karna padta hai na?*'

She paused, and I could almost hear the irritation in her voice when she replied, '*Tu kar leta hoga. Main nahi kar pa rahi.*'

'*Kar nahi pa rahi ya karna nahi chahti ho?*' The words slipped out sharper than I intended.

There was a moment of silence on the other end. Maybe she hadn't expected me to be this blunt. Maybe I hadn't either. But it was out there now, hanging between us, waiting for her response.

There was a slight shift in her tone, something defensive. '*Main tumhari* girlfriend *nahi hoon jo roz tumhare liye* time *nikaalun,*' she said, almost like she wanted to put up a wall between us.

I felt a pang in my chest, but I stayed calm. 'I know,' I replied, my voice steady, 'but last year *bhi toh tum meri* girlfriend *nahi thi,* right? *Phir tab kyun baat hoti thi roz?*'

She sighed, as if she had already thought of this answer. '*Wo tum apni marzi se baat karte the, apne* consent *se.* I didn't ask for it.'

I paused, her words sinking in. I wanted to say more, but she didn't give me the chance.

'*Ab mere paas* time *nahi hai.* I'm busy, and I need time for myself. Last year *itna kuch nahi tha mere paas karne ko.*'

Her words felt colder than they probably were meant to. But they hit me hard, and, for a moment, I had no idea what to say.

She was right. Friendship didn't come with a rulebook, and it didn't require daily conversations. I wasn't her boyfriend, and I had no right to expect her to call me regularly. That wasn't part of the deal.

'Yeah,' I mumbled, more to myself than to her. 'I'm not your boyfriend. Why would you need to talk to me every day?'

But deep down, it stung. Because even though we weren't in a relationship, it had felt like we were something . . . more. Or maybe I had just convinced myself of that.

Now, she didn't need to call me.

'*Chor ye sab,*' she sighed, her voice tired, almost frustrated.

'*Nahi*,' I interrupted, my tone firmer than I intended. 'It's hurting me.'

'Hurting what?' she snapped back, confusion and irritation laced in her words. 'I never gave you any hope. I never said anything like that.'

I paused for a moment, feeling numb. 'So, I was just a time pass for you, right?'

'No!' She shouted back. 'I spoke to you like a friend, that's all.'

'For God's sake, come on; please stop this,' she begged now with low tones, almost as if imploring me to let it go. '*Tu apne* placements *par dhyan de,* and I'll focus on my life too. We both have so much going on.'

Still feeling numb, I forced out an answer, 'Hmm . . . okay.'

'And yeah, I'm off now. I have a class at eight in the morning,' she said. 'We'll talk sometime later.'

Desperation crept into my voice, 'Five more minutes? Can't we talk for just five minutes?'

'No,' she declared firmly, and that finality was like a brick coming on my head.

'Good night,' she said, and the line was dead before I could have any response.

I looked at the screen—nineteen minutes and twelve seconds. Calls that would go on for hours—those long-parlored conversations of two and half hours—turned into mere minutes.

After the call, I sat there and looked at the phone, the weight of everything pressing down on me internally. I just had this sense of drowning in questions and doubt and an emptiness that I couldn't get my head around.

Was she right? Or, had I crossed some invisible line? The questions circled around my mind like a storm I was unable to escape.

I wondered if I was the one who had spoiled it, by confessing my feelings, by wanting things to not change and stay the same.

I opened WhatsApp and typed, my fingers shaking as the words spilled out: 'I can't do this anymore, Tanishka. It's not even about my feelings for you . . . it's about something more. Last year, I was the same—busy, stressed, drowning in things I had to do. But I still made time for you. Not because it was convenient, but because you mattered to me. And now, I feel like I don't matter at all, I just want your friendship the way it was before, if not then let's end this, let's not be best friends anymore . . .!'

I stared at the message. I must have reread it a dozen times, feeling my heart pounding in my chest while I fought the urge to just delete the whole thing. But I didn't. I pressed the send button, for in those few words, something had changed between us, perhaps irreversibly.

The message was delivered, and there I was, staring at it, waiting. Waiting for what? I didn't know. Maybe for her to understand. Maybe to care. Maybe just for an indication that everything I felt was not in vain. But waiting didn't really help; the longer I waited, the heavier that silence felt.

I just wanted to be in her life, as I always had been, to matter in the way I once did. Her presence made me happy—*not because I wanted something more,* but because just knowing she was there made everything else in life a little easier to bear.

Sometimes, it's not about holding someone close, but knowing that they're out there, existing, and that's enough to keep your heart from breaking completely.

But by that time, the night had dragged on longer than I could stand. I held my breath, wishing for anything, anything at all. Did she come to see how badly I wanted things to be okay between us, how much I missed the way we were?

And the next day, my phone buzzed:

'Okay, as you wish so . . . Can we be strangers again?'

And then, all at once, everything seemed to come off; the last thread had snapped.

I was expecting something different. Something that would tell me she understood, that maybe she still cared in the way I hoped. Instead, I was just that friend whose absence wouldn't leave a mark. *Maybe, I was just a fleeting chapter in her story, one that had to end for her to move forward. While she was my whole book, I was merely a few pages she could easily turn past.*

The Weight of What's Left

As I am sitting here today, holding her keychain, my eyes slowly fill up with tears whilst I think back on everything. I keep hoping, wishing for a chance for all the visions to come together.

Amid all these things, I didn't know what to do. Each day seemed like a hill on either side of which were the endless gorges of holding on and letting things go. I kept on waiting by the phone praying, wishing for a text, a call—silence.

Meanwhile, life went on. Stumbling through classes, assignments, exam pressure and just the pressure of final placements in play, everything became a bit of a blur, as if I were going through the motions of life, my mind still churning somewhere in the past, trying to figure out a puzzle that had no solution.

I had friends who understood me, people who would try to fill that void. But no matter how hard they tried, the void couldn't ultimately dissipate the weight of her absence. *How do you move on from someone who once meant everything, and is now a memory, just a stranger wearing the face of someone you used to know?*

As the weeks ticked by, everything got jolted by the whirlwind of campus placements. October arrived, along with the make-or-break rush to justify the twenty-lakh fees we had shelled out for our degrees. There was chaos—placement week was underway. Companies flooded the campus. Inboxes became a battlefield of CVs and shortlist confirmations, and I finally got my first break on 7 October.

I didn't know whether to feel relieved or more nervous. The nights were no longer about sleep; they were about mock interviews, rehearsing answers, trying not to sound like a robot but also not to mess up the one chance I had. That whole night, I was stuck in a cycle of reciting questions, anticipating what they might ask. By morning, I looked like a zombie, but no time for that—I had to get into Western business formals, clean-shaven (which I absolutely hated).

The day was a marathon. First, it was an aptitude test, a ruthless group discussion and, as if I hadn't been put through enough, two rounds of intense interviews. By the time I reached the final round, my heart was doing laps, and I was functioning on sheer adrenaline. But then, it happened.

Then, it happened.

When the Placement Committee member called my name, I didn't know what to expect. She looked at me, smiled and said, 'You got placed.'

For a second, I just stood there. It was everything I'd worked for, all the late nights, all the stress—it had led to this. Without a second thought, I hugged her right then and there before everybody. The recruiters, the candidates—they all saw it, but I didn't care at the time.

As I walked out of there, I felt like I was floating. I called my parents right away, their voices on the other end a combination of pride and happiness. Then, before I even realized it, I started thinking about Tanishka. Without thinking, I typed, 'Hey, I got placed.' I clicked 'send'. . . and then, something held me back. A sudden hesitation. I glanced at the message, and a wave of uncertainty washed over me. I deleted it.

I didn't know why I did it, but I couldn't reach out to her—not like this. Something had shifted, maybe it was the quiet realization that some things just aren't meant to be rekindled. I remembered when I first got into IIM Goa—I'd called her before anyone else. She was the one I'd wanted to share everything with. Now, something stopped me.

Sometimes, the hardest part isn't letting go; it's accepting that the person you once turned to first is now a stranger.

Days went by, and again, on the fourteenth, I finally learned to feel less excited about my day. The hours rolled on, with heartbeats reaching a frenzied pace at each of the notifications, wondering if perhaps it was she. The phone calls and texts were incessantly awaited, longing for Tanishka's message. But the heart of the night struck with more clarity, and I felt the quiet pain of her absence.

Somewhere in the night, two in the morning, I went out to the balcony, the same balcony that every past memory seemed to take my heart to. Sitting down, puffing a cigarette, I thought to myself while the smoke rose high into a star-studded sky—as someone once said—'ll wait for her. I'll wait till my lungs are filled with ashes.'

But worse than the waiting were the relentless loops of 'what if' that played in my mind like an unbroken song. If I could go back, would I have held on tighter? Would I have told her more about how special she was to me? Sometimes, it is hardest to deal with the fact that you gave it your best shot and still wonder if it was enough.

Suddenly, my phone buzzed, bringing me back to life with a surprise. A missed call from an unknown number made my heart leap—could it be her?

I picked up holding my breath to hear a familiar voice through that line. 'Hello,' she said softly. It was Avantika.

I pondered, for a moment, whether to carry on now. Part of me hesitated, not being sure if this union was worth it. But strangely, I felt slightly pacified; maybe I didn't hold any grudge against her anymore. The hurt had dulled, yet it hadn't healed. But I didn't hate her.

'Happy Birthday,' she said, her voice gentle, almost cautious.

'Thanks,' I replied, with a quiet smile she couldn't see. It felt strange yet comforting, like finding an old photograph you'd forgotten existed.

There was a pause, and then she asked, 'How have you been? It's . . . been a while.'

'Yeah, it has,' I replied, my voice steady. 'Life's been busy, I guess. Gotten used to some changes . . . you know how it is.'

She laughed softly, a sound I hadn't heard in ages. 'Yeah, I do.' Then, almost hesitantly, she said, 'I'm sorry again. I should have been honest about things from the start.'

'It's okay. I've moved on,' I said, wondering how true it felt. 'I don't have anything for you anymore . . . not the way that I did.'

She paused for a moment, and then said, her tone gentle but full of weight. 'Life moves fast, doesn't it? One moment, we're making future plans together and the next moment, we're strangers on opposite sides of the line.'

I had to ask, 'How's Mehul? The one you used to keep from the world . . . and from me.'

There was a little sigh on the other end. 'We're not in touch anymore.'

I thought about asking 'why', but before I could, she added, 'Maybe we all just play the roles we're meant to. Some people come into our lives to stay, and others . . . maybe they're just there to point us in the right direction. Honestly . . . I've learned a lot because of you and because of Mehul as well.'

Her words hit harder than I expected, like an ache I thought I'd buried. I couldn't help but wonder if this was how it would end with Tanishka too. Just another story, another stranger I'd eventually let go. No . . . I didn't want that. I didn't want her to just be part of my past.

Avantika snapped at me, 'Hey, are you still there?'

I steadied myself and cleared my throat, 'Yes, I am here.'

What she said—her words—were hauntingly true. 'Yes, you might be right. Maybe, that is what strangers really are. Guides in disguise, showing us parts of ourselves that we would not be able to see on our own,' I replied.

She fell silent for a moment and then asked softly, 'And . . . How is Tanishka?'

I hesitated, unwilling to share too much. 'She's . . . fine. Everything's fine. Take care, Avantika,' I said, carrying a sense of closure but free of bitterness.

'You too,' she replied softly. 'Maybe, someday, our paths will cross again . . . even if it's like strangers.'

As the call ended, a strange blend of closure and curiosity lingered. I stepped back into my room and left the door open—a quiet invitation to the unknown, to whatever or whoever might step through and take me away, freeing me.

The night came and brought with its darkness, the weight of all those whom I have held and lost. I realised that life is an endless cycle of arrivals and farewells, of both those who are strangers or mirrors to what we seek. Somewhere, in the midst of it all, there was Tanishka—a name, a memory, a question that lingered like an unfinished story.

Maybe this was the beginning of a new journey, one where every stranger held a piece of my past and a glimpse of my future, waiting to unfold.

Life has a way of leading us to where we need to be, even if it's with strangers.

Strangers are just familiar souls who meet us at the crossroads of who we were and who we're meant to be.

The end

Acknowledgement

Writing this book has been a journey filled with emotions, growth and countless rewrites. I couldn't have done it alone, and I don't want to pretend otherwise.

First, to **Priyam Agarwal,** thank you for reading this book not once, not twice, but ten times. Your patience, dedication and honesty kept me grounded throughout this process. You caught every little detail I missed and made this journey so much easier. This book wouldn't have been half of what it is without you.

To **Manav Goyal,** thank you for all the ideas, the brainstorming sessions and for making and shooting the reel that brought this book to life in a whole new way. Also, for the last-minute edits and ensuring everything came together perfectly.

To **Bhavya Kaila,** one of the first readers of this book, thank you for your suggestions that made it better. And I'll never forget how we both cried on the second-last page—those moments made it all worth it.

To **Aastha Asati**, you've been here from the very beginning. From the first scribbles to the final chapter, you stayed through every high and low.

Lastly, thank you to everyone who picked up this book. I hope it stays with you the way it stayed with me while writing it.

Scan QR code to access the
Penguin Random House India website